666

A collection of 32 horror fantabbles from around the globe

First Published 2016 by Fantastic Books Publishing

Cover design and artwork by Dean Samed

ISBN (ebook): 978-1-909163-99-7
ISBN (paperback): 978-1-909163-16-4

DEDICATION

To anyone who has ever sat around a camp fire or huddled in a tent with a torch, telling tales of terror to delight their friends and family.

This collection is for you.

ACKNOWLEDGEMENTS

With huge thanks to everyone whose work appears in this collection including our invited contributors Michael Brookes, Nathan Robinson, John Scotcher, Regina Puckett, Stuart Aken and Linda Acaster.

We adore your work and although horrific, your stories delighted us in equal measure.

NOTE FROM THE PUBLISHER

A Fantabble is a story of exactly 666 words and the authors featured in this anthology have excelled in their execution of this arduous and mind bending task. I salute each and every one of them.

From Poe's *The Raven* to Lovecraft's *The Call of Cthulhu*, Layman's *The Cellar* to King's *The Shining*, we have all been made to shudder at a finely written horror tale and the stories herein are no exception.

10% of the proceeds of this title will be donated to the Freedom from Torture charity, an organisation that deals with the rehabilitation of people who have suffered real horror in their lives. Thank you for purchasing your copy and helping this worthy organisation to continue its vital and sadly necessary role in the world.

FOREWORD BY MICHAEL BROOKES

666 is one of the most well-known numbers in Western horror tradition. Everyone recognises it from the Book of Revelations as the beginning of the end of the world. It has become a symbol for the birth of the ultimate evil, and of the final battle between heaven and hell. It's no surprise that with such a rich context it forms the core of many horror stories, and it's a tale that continues to entice.

For this particular anthology, the number has an additional meaning, as each of the stories is exactly 666 words long. These are bite-sized morsels of terror from a diverse selection of authors. Some are already known favourites of Fantastic Books Publishing, others have demonstrated their talent by winning contests, and a few – myself included – were invited to take part.

The horror genre covers a wide range of stories, and each of this anthology's authors brings something new. I'm honoured to have one of my stories included and I hope you enjoy it, along with all the other tales on offer.

Michael

CONTENTS

The Tree of Nails by Michael Brookes

Headhunted by John Hoggard

A Prologue by Rose Thurlbeck

Under The Fig Tree by Brad Greenwood

The Needle and the Camel's Eye by Rose Thurlbeck

Bad Vibrations at Stratisfest by Denise Hayes

The Sands of Time by Ann Bupryn

What's That Sniffing at My Window in the Middle of the Night by Rose Thurlbeck

Loft Conversion by Denise Hayes

The Perfect Family by Kester Park

Entombed by Ulla & Marko Susimetsa

The Sufferers by Jack Mann

A Perfect Match by Denise Hayes

Jumping at Shadows by Jx Plant

The Number of the Beast by Celia Coyne

His Spectre by John Scotcher

Assisted by Richard Dixon

The Statue in the Playground by Darren Grey

The In-Terror-Gator by Isla Sandford Hall

Facing Up by Richard Dixon

Parents Evening by CM Angus

Can This Day Possibly Get Any Worse by Regina Puckett

Opening Doors by Penny Grubb

Music at Full Moon by Melodie Trudeaux

From The Depths by Chris Chambers

Three Wishes Jack by Carmody Lanes

The Gnome House by Fortune Selles

A Walk In The Wood by Mark P Henderson

The Pond by Denise Hayes

She Sings only at Night by Nathan Robinson

Ouija by Stuart Aken

Number Thirteen by Linda Acaster

The Tree of Nails by Michael Brookes

The tree stood alone, ancient and withered, stark against the setting sun. Its roots emanated a sweet fragrance of decay. Once dense forest carpeted this area, long since whittled down over the centuries through farming and ship building. For generations, farmers had tried to nurture crops in the surrounding fields, but even the hardiest weeds and grass failed to grow here. It no longer resembled the mighty oak it once was. The incarceration took as great a toll on the prison as it did on the prisoner.

And the prisoner was the last of his kind, and so a rarity in this modern age. Not that he knew of the monumental changes the world had seen. He'd once lived in the forest, feasting on those that dwelt there. He'd once possessed a name, a true name, but even he couldn't remember it now. He was a spirit spawned from the dark side of nature. His memories of those joyous times pained him now, but the pain didn't compare to that caused by the spell for a thousand years.

It was Artair, the Saxon sorcerer, who used Woden's power to imprison him. Although the magician was long dead, his spell remained potent. The spirit sensed only a suggestion of the world beyond the tree. Despite this, he gained hope during his imprisonment. All spirits have power, even trapped ones. Especially trapped ones. When pierced with iron and blood it provided a link to the outside world, and in doing so, granted prophetic visions to the supplicant.

He'd known the witches of the forest and from the surrounding hills. Their devilry often approached his own, and as practitioners of the dark arts they knew the signs of the wood.

More than that, they knew their meaning. Around the tree they conducted their rituals of sex and violence. They hammered nails through their sacrifices into the wood. Even now, the tree's flesh was riddled with rusty marks, almost as if it were diseased.

The legend of the tree spread, and the rituals balanced the lonely days with magical nights. But as the seasons passed, the intervals between the visitations stretched further apart, and so too did those brief moments of bliss. Eventually, they were almost lost amongst the horror of his constant suffering. The pulp of the tree smothered his howls of rage and despair, and so became twisted in sympathy.

Decades passed in dreadful solitude until one dark night, when the moon was barely a sliver in the sky, he sensed a fluttering heartbeat. The same heartbeat created music for him now as it approached once again with that characteristic unsteady gait. She'd visited many times over the past months. He couldn't see her, not properly, but snatched glimpses of her body and soul in the brief transactions. He learned her name was Rachel, although he knew little of her except her desires to punish others.

Like her schemes, her offerings were pitiful, scraps of animal life barely worth the term, and she lacked the vitality of the covens of old. They knew the value of sacrifice, and how to satisfy his lusts and hunger. But she knew enough of the old ways to make the blood count. Her wishes were self-centred, but as his only avenue for escape he encouraged her with terrible visions. Those that had wronged her in slight, unintended ways would perish in the cruelest fashion. With whispers he promised those futures to her, knowing that from her meagre gifts he would claw his way free.

He heard a rabbit's squeal, and a hammer pounding nails into the tree, and thence into his flesh. The iron pierced him and he screamed. The blood, weak as it was, granted a moment of strength. He cast a vision to Rachel of a co-worker crushed into mangled flesh. The euphoria soon faded, but as she walked away, still smiling at the death to come, she failed to see the widening crack in the bark of the tree.

About the Author

Michael Brookes, Executive Producer with a leading UK games developer, lists his two life passions as working in games and writing, and considers himself fortunate to be able to indulge them both. He enjoys the starry skies of east England where he lives and, when not at work or writing, he sometimes sleeps. This is good because sleep is the origin of many of his best ideas. Michael is an invited contributor to this anthology.

Headhunted by John Hoggard

Bob arrived with a huge delivery truck on Washington plates. As it was unloaded he told me he was brought in from Seattle; boasted he'd been headhunted. I nodded, but said nothing, hoping he'd go away and leave me be. He did eventually; when the truck left, climbing into his shiny Buick and heading off to his new office.

When Fall temperatures dipped and the first frosts came I started spending less time outside and my awkward moments with boastful Bob became less frequent. I was grateful for the respite.

I did worry that Bob never tried to fit into our community. Perhaps I never really gave him a chance. As I prepared for Halloween, he came home early one cold evening. He laughed at my pumpkin carving. 'You don't even have kids!' he said, loudly and unnecessarily.

'I know,' I replied, barely looking up, concentrating on the patterns emerging beneath the tip of my sharp knife.

Bob tutted and went inside, the screen door slamming in the quietness of the street.

'Not any more,' I whispered into the gloom after he'd gone. 'None of us do.'

I think perhaps I felt a little guilty that evening. It wasn't Bob's fault, after all. It's not like I'd ever explained... Then again, Bob had not struck me as the kind of man who would have believed me if I told him the truth.

I finished carving my own pumpkins, their faces twisted and terrifying. It was then I decided to carve two for Bob, one for each door. It would be difficult to explain their importance but I would try.

I carved into the night and fell asleep some time before dawn. When I awoke, the sun was up and Bob had already left for work. I prepared a note for him, which I had to rewrite many times because I didn't want to scare him or for him to think me insane, but he needed to understand.

I placed my guardians on his porch, pinned the note to his door at eye height and retired back to my own yard, carefully setting out my lanterns, carefully avoiding eye contact with my neighbours, who were setting out their own protection.

In the dying embers of sunlight I began to light the candles in my carved pumpkin guardians. It was dark by the time I had finished and Bob was not home – his guardians remained unilluminated. I hovered at my doorway, but I couldn't risk it. I closed the door and waited.

When Bob returned, the street was alive with flickering orange lights. There was a long pause between the slam of his car door and the clatter of his screen. I had high hopes he had read the note and acted upon my advice, but when I risked a quick glance, his porch remained dark.

I retired to the cupboard under the stairs and waited.

When they came, their incessant tapping and whispering was temporarily drowned by my own involuntarily whimpering. They stopped right outside my yard and I bit my lip hard to silence myself, but my guardians were fearsome and many, and I sensed their retreat.

They did not go far, for the old Ferguson place, now Bob's place, was unprotected. I scrunched up my eyes and held my breath, the pain from my screaming lungs drowning out their hypnotic calls to go outside.

A screen door slammed.

The tapping and whispering stopped.

I knew they were gone for another year.

I sobbed with guilt and relief.

The police came round on the afternoon of the second. They peered through the windows of Bob's house, pushed over a softening pumpkin with a boot. They asked me about Bob. They said he hadn't been at work for two days. I shrugged, said I hadn't seen him since Halloween.

'Perhaps he's been headhunted again,' I said as the two officers returned to their car. 'Lots of folk round here are,' I added quietly as they drove away.

About the Author

This story was highly commended by the judges of our horror competition. John has been writing for as long as he can remember, his first publishing successes coming in the Hartlepool Mail "Chipper Club" when he was six. Since then he has continued to write mainly in the science fiction and fantasy genres, winning prizes for his 'fan-fic' of the Star Trek franchise in his twenties at the various conventions he attended.

John's work also appears in our Sci-Fi anthologies Fusion and Synthesis.

Find out more about John and his work over on the WordWatchers website at www.wordwatchers.net.

A Prologue by Rose Thurlbeck

Thursday 11th February 02:35

He's asleep and I am a husk. I have nothing left to say for myself–

What's that you say, sister? Let me tell you a story...

Damn. No. Shut up. I'm here to talk about me, not listen to you. This is my diary, my space to talk about me. Me, me, me. Just me, not you.

I hear you. I gazed into the eyes of the marble Medusa...

No. Go away.

Yep. The creatures we encountered in the waters of the ocean moon...

I'm too tired.

You got it, Toots. I had to die three times to get away...

Please.

You got moxie, kid. If the angel hadn't cried, I never would have understood...

It's all about me.

Not really. The day the MacGuffin was delivered, I don't know who was more surprised, me or the mailman...

Me.

No, you weren't there, I would have remembered. Anyway, the envelope was warm – warmer than you'd expect it to be, even on a hot day – and the mailman asked me what was in it–

Me.

Are you even listening? I just said you weren't there, and the content of the mysterious package was not... Jeez, kid. I don't mind telling you these stories, and you working them up for your readers, but we got a deal, remember?

Me.

Kid you're beginning to really piss me off, now. Let me finish my story, then I'll get out of your hair.

No.

I don't even know where to begin with that. Have you ever considered seeing someone about–

Me.

You. It's just you. Always about you, and all the time 'Ooh, I'm so depressed. Ooh, I have no friends, nobody cares. I'm going to end up dying on my own.'

Me.

Yeah, you. Except you won't be on your own will yah? I'll be there, too.

Really?

Of course I will, kid. I'll be the one standing over you with the knife in my hand and your blood pooling out over the floor, and I'll get to finish my story because you won't be able to interrupt me.

But you'll be killing yourself as well. Being part of me, I mean.

And the last thing you hear will be my voice telling you what Hell is really like as the curtains close on your pathetic little life.

I created you...

I am grateful. I am the fruit of your imagination, the guy with the gangster spiel. I am that magical moment all authors experience when their characters come to life and start talking back to their creator.

I just never shut up again, did I?

...so I can destroy you.

How's that working out for yah? Listen, kid. The truth is, without me you'd be nuthin', your career – well, there's no books, and without books an author is just another dreamer, and they're a dime a bag at the pick'n'mix. So let's write some stories. Scary stories.

I don't write horror.

Kid, I learned this new trick. Feel that? That's me smiling. That crack in the back of your skull is my grin. Don't make me laugh, kid.

But I don't. It's all blood and people being mean to each other.

You write what I tell you, then you pretty it up. I start a story 'the prisoner was alone in his cell at the top of the tower,' you can be all... well?

The White Tower lances the sky, its shadow flung across the valley like that of a sundial's gnomon.

The fuck. What's a gnomon?

Guess.

Anyway, that's our deal. I give you the characters, the stories. You paint the pictures. And no blood, I promise. Well, maybe just one drop.

You know, if you ever have kids, bedtimes will be all, "Once upon a time when the world was young and magic filled the air..."

No. They'll be, 'Hey buddy, if you want a story before you go to sleep, you'd better settle down real quick.'

'Once upon a time...'

Shut up.

About the Author

Dark Rose wrote some stories –
counting one, two, three.
Fresh, she picked them
red and succulent,
from the Hanging Tree.

Twitter: @Garthyre
Pronounce
to rhyme
with
fear

Bobby's lunch of cheese sticks and rice crackers rattled in his miniature backpack. He bounced along humming something to himself. *What was that tune?* Gareth thought.

The rattle stopped in front of the gates to Centennial Park and Bobby yanked his baby fist out of his father's hand and started talking to his friend.

Gareth splashed latte on his tie. 'Bobby, keep moving… We're gonna be late.' But Bobby's mouth just flapped, spurting nonsense, his gaze fixed on the thin air beside him. 'Bobby!'

'Dad, my friend says we should take a short cut.'

'Let me guess… through the park? Past the playground?' Gareth asked, suppressing a smile.

'Yeah!' Bobby hollered.

'Don't get excited we've got to go straight to school.' Gareth warned.

He held his son's hand and listened to the rhythmic thump of cheese sticks in Tupperware. 'Hey Bobby what was that song you keep singing?'

Bobby rolled his eyes in a theatrical gesture. 'I don't know, something *he* taught me, it's about a weepy tree.' Bobby hummed a bar and Gareth's thoughts rolled back to a time when he had his own secret friend like Bobby's.

The first day Gareth met Daniel it was beneath a tree just like the giant figs that grew near the playground. He was eight years old again beneath that tree rounding the knotted trunk. Wet grass and mossy stains climbed over the roots. He was busting, so he took a piss behind the ancient trunk.

While he was doing his business he examined the scars etched in the bark. There was a crude love heart carved between the names *Jenny and Jack*. He zipped up and followed the narrative around the tree. There was a *HI* freshly gouged into the trunk. Gareth remembered thinking that was stupid. Hi? What kind of statement was that? He moved on dragging his fingers across the rough skin as he circled the tree, reading its tattoos. *Benny sucks balls. Johnny D wuz here. Stop pissing on me you cock smoker* made him giggle and his cheeks flush.

Dappled light sparkled on the tree's grey skin. The leaves above rustled and for a moment the breeze carried a strange tune. He wandered around the tree in a trance, passed *Jenny for Jack* once more, passed the freshly gouged *HI G!* Gareth felt the juice in his veins turn to ice. The message had changed. Was that G for Gareth? He looked about. Not a soul. He went round again. *Jack and Jenny* still frozen in time. Round the bend once more.

'Dad, look at that big tree!' Before Gareth could stop him, Bobby was hanging from an old rope dangling from a low branch.

In Gareth's mind he was still eight years old, rounding that bend, his heart pounding. *HI G! WANT TA PLAY? DANIEL.* The cut so fresh it wept with sap.

Gareth wanted to play. This time he started round and quickly doubled back, hoping to catch the culprit. He thought he saw a shadow whip around the other side of the trunk and chased it. Round and round he went.

Bobby giggled and chatted excitedly to his friend!

'Bobby, get back here!' Gareth's fear expanded with his memories of that day. His breathless eight-year-old self read the fresh carving aloud. *WANNA SEE ME* it said. He remembered rounding that fig one more time to find the words *LOOK UP.*

He heard the creaking of the tightening rope before he saw Daniel hanging from it. His limp body swayed in the shadow of the fig. Sunlight glinted off his milky, open eyes. He seemed to be smiling. A weak whistle gurgled from his blue lips reciting a familiar tune. Much later Gareth would discover it was a song from a movie… something about a weeping tree.

Gareth gripped his son's shoulders but it was too late.

Bobby's head was tilted skyward, and there under the fig, etched in the trunk were the words Gareth had tried to forget. *LOOK UP.*

About the Author

Brad began work in the Australian film industry after graduating from the Queensland College of Art in 1990 and he has built an impressive CV, having contributed as a designer and artist to many projects including Peter Jackson's Lord of the Rings, George Miller's Happy Feet and Zack Snyder's Legend of the Guardians. He also art directed the animated film Blinky Bill. Brad also features in Fantastic Books' Sci-Fi anthology, Fusion.

The Needle and the Camel's Eye by Rose Thurlbeck

The White Tower lances the sky, its shadow flung across the valley like that of a sundial's gnomon. From high, the prisoner looks out, hoping to catch the flash of sunlight on steel as novice fighters – his lads – go through their exercises among the ruined cloisters that crown the hill opposite. Two things distract him: the sweep of the shadow across the landscape toward the hour of his execution, and the stubborn, unrelenting, wet thump, thump, thump from his neighbour's wall.

The door opens and his jailer enters. 'It is today.'

'Tell me – what is today?

'The day the will of the court is executed.'

'When "life by the mercy of the needle, death by the guidance of the camel's eye" was pronounced, its meaning was never made clear to me. I am a stranger here and you are my last friend. Explain it to me. And do something about *that!*'

Thump. Thump. Thump.

'I can do neither.'

The prisoner turns away from the window. 'What should I expect?'

'I don't know.'

'Please. I know that this' – he spreads his arms – 'is surely the needle, but the camel's eye?'

The jailer shakes his head. 'This is The White Tower. The condemned is alone with his Executor. No one can know what occurs between them, it is sacred. After, your cell is open and none will stop you leaving.'

'Then I live? This makes no sense to me.'

'Did you ever hear of Petrello? The artist?'

The prisoner turns back to the window. 'Another story?'

'He was the best in the Kingdom, known for the detail of his brushwork. The King commissioned from him *The Goddess Anthelopone Weeping For The Death Of Her Son,* and when it was delivered hung it in the summer palace. Petrello boasted it was his self portrait, but no-one believed him.

It was the youngest princess that saw it first. She was fascinated by the picture, stared at it for hours like it was some kind of puzzle, 'til she suddenly starts giggling. The King wondered what was so funny, but all she could do was point at the goddess in all her mournfulness. So the King looked and there, sitting on an eyelash is a single tear reflecting the scene in front of the painting including the artist standing by his canvas holding his palette and brushes, completely naked and with a massive erection. As I said, known for his detail.'

'The needle was his reward?'

The jailer nodded. 'He lost the use of his fingers, then his hands. When he learned to paint with his feet, that ability was taken from him. He's stubborn, and he even learns to paint with his mouth. Took him years.'

'A determined man.'

'He's an artist. He has to create, much like you must destroy.'

'Go on.'

'The needle continues its work, so now he can't eat properly, can't talk. But he needs to paint. So he does what he can, with such materials he has.'

The wet thumping noise fills the sudden silence. The guard looks at the prisoner. 'For now the needle is merciful.'

The shadow sweeps on. The waiting prisoner hears the step of a stranger ascending the stairs, long before he hears her whispers.

The woman entering his cell is dressed in black, white bindings scattered with red rosebuds at her wrists. Her hands are empty, her eyes lined with a pain long held. She does not look at him, but slowly unties the knot below her left thumb.

As the linen unwinds, the flowers there bloom, scentless but vivid scarlet, petals opening to welcome another day until at last with a little pull the cloth comes away from the three needles piercing the veins at her bloody wrist. Still whispering, the woman gently extracts one unwilling needle, dragging a drop of blood from the opening to hang dancing from the point.

The prisoner kneels, the whispering woman tends the eye and the needle is guided home.

About the Author

Rose Thurlbeck plans to explore the world of the White Tower again, if she remembers the way. This – the second Dark Rose story in this anthology – is dedicated to the author Tanith Lee (1947-2015).

singsixpence.blogspot.com

Bad Vibrations at StratisFest by Denise Hayes

Some people would kill for a ticket to StratisFest. It has the most amazing lineup – top DeathManga bands from Earth, DarkDjent combos from Moon Colony and the best AltAlien music. Say what you like about the stomach-turning ugliness of the Kapteyn girlbands, the weird setup of their vocal folds creates a SupraThresh vibrato that plays all kinds of crazy tricks on your brain (and other body parts).

The gig only happens every three years when Space Facility L0T1 has a complete makeover. The way this run-of-the-mill maintenance-base is blinged-up is legendary. You name it, Stratisfest apparently has it: thirty-metre rainbow-coloured waterfalls circling Stadium 1; laser-light projections that turn the Earth into a giant glitterball; and – when the music stops – individual YurtDomes to crash in.

Of course there'll be downsides – the kind you get at any festival where mainlining and free-screwing are pretty compulsory. Not everyone comes home intact. But I'm happy to burn my candle at both ends.

That's why I'm risking gatecrashing the gig. Once again, I got unlucky ticket-wise but – as they say – money talks. The kind of wallet-busting conversations I've had got me here on the Spacebus via a service chute and into a reserve LifePod in the storage sector. When we arrive, I'll slip into the disembarkation queue, cool as you like. I didn't go through the official registration process before boarding but that shouldn't be a problem: security is – I'm told – pretty lax after takeoff. There's no need for wristbands in space. And I've heard there're always empty seats on the way back.

I set the Pod to Destination AutoMode and close my eyes. Stratisfest here I come!

I'm woken from my inflight dreams by my Pod alarm and sneak up to the passenger deck. Everyone here seems pretty zoned-out. I guess the pill-party started as soon as the Pods popped. Still, it suits me that no-one's up for conversation. Safer that way.

The queue marches, zombie-fashion, down the exit ramp and into a huge receiving area. It's grim - cold, grey and utilitarian. We're met by festival stewards who, oddly enough, are all Kapteyn women. The stench from their oozing exo-organs makes them even more revolting in the flesh than on screen. No wonder theirs is an endangered species. The Kapteyn males must just lie back and think of the planet – especially if space-ranger folklore is to be believed. The story goes that the females' way of getting jiggy is so radical they kill half the males they get it on with. Sexy, yeah?

We're channeled into a narrow passageway. Just up ahead are three band members from Dreadshift. At the front of the queue, near what must be the entrance to the festival arena, two Kapteyn women are handing out VR headsets. Every now and then, though, the odd guy (including Dreadshift's drummer) is pulled out of line and siphoned off through a side-door.

Now it's my turn. The women look me up and down, licking their slimy lips, then I'm pushed into a brightly-lit annex. Bad vibes here, man. Naked Kapteyn women line the sidewalls. On the wall ahead are four manacles; two at shoulder height, two – wide apart – for the ankles. Just to the left of these is the Dreadshift guy, slumped unconscious in a pool of blood. A female approaches me. As she gets closer, a weird appendage, scaly and edged with bony barbs, emerges from between her legs.

She must see in my eyes that I'm fully aware and totally terrified. She shrieks something in Kapteyn then a syringe is plunged into my neck and a VR set rammed on my head. I struggle blindly as I'm grabbed from all sides, stripped and spread-eagled on the wall.

Then the drugs kick in and the VR show begins and everything's cool.

I see in pixilated splendour the glittering spinning Earth, DeathManga screams pierce my eardrums, and the spray from a thousand waterfalls runs in warm rivulets down my thighs.

To die for, man.

About the Author

Denise taught Creative Writing for many years but now enjoys being able to focus on her own work. She writes poetry and prose and is inspired by facts, jokes and her favourite authors J.G. Ballard, Jorge Luis Borges and Philip K Dick.

She has published poems in Myslexia and other magazines and flash fiction in the Salt anthology Overheard: Stories to Read

Aloud. When she's not writing she's in her converted cellar painting, printing and making odd little dioramas in tins.

Denise runs the Twitter project twitter.com/Gregueria1 and blogs on all things creative at;

rosecottagedennysaze.blogspot.co.uk and

dennysaze.blogspot.co.uk.

'That man's climbing our way. I don't think we should wait here, Dix.'

'Why not? We've as much right here as anyone.'

'Yeah but Dix, he's dead creepy. Where's Kathryn? We promised to keep an eye on her.'

'I'm here, Charlotte. Who's that man?'

'Dix! Look how quick he's climbing.'

'Dix…?'

'Come on, Charlotte… Kathryn. Run!'

'Okay, stop. He can't follow us here. Charlotte, let me have a go on your game. You said I could.'

'I said *if* we see them, you can, but not on the beach. I don't want sand in it.'

'Will we see them? I'm scared.'

'Shut up, Kathryn. If you're going to act like a kid, go home.'

'But will we? Will they have magic?'

'That's fairy-tale rubbish, Kathryn. I'm fed up of you always following us.'

'I don't. I've not come with you before.'

'She's right, she hasn't, Dix. This is the first time.'

'Well it feels like you've been following us for years, whining.'

'I don't, do I, Charlotte?'

'I suppose not. Still, I know what Dix means. We might see them if there's a crowd. That's what Kathryn's mum said.'

'I've never seen them, and I live here.'

'There's that man again. What's he doing?'

'Wooo... He creeps and clambers... Searching and seeking for his long lost daughter...'

'You're scaring me, Charlotte!'

'Charlotte, did Kathryn's mum say Kathryn's grandma had seen them?'

'No, but she knew a woman who had when she was little, in Edwardian times.'

'What's Edwardian times?'

'It means wearing funny togs.'

'Where did they come from? A spaceship?'

'She says they came walking out of the rocks, dressed funny and carrying the magic box.'

'Was she scared?'

'Not at first, but then the others came and they turned nasty, shouting and casting spells, and they all ran off.'

'I don't want you to run off, Dix. You've got to look after me.'

'That man's there again. He looks like your dad, Kathryn.'

'He doesn't! He's too old.'

'What's he doing, Dix?'

'I'm scared. I want to go home.'

'Baby!'

'I'm not, Dix, but my dad says I wasn't to stay out late. I want to go home.'

'We've only been out for five minutes.'

'Well, I think we've been out for years and years and I want to go home, so there!'

'Shut up Kathryn. I wish that man wasn't always here when there's just us. Come on, let's climb up.'

'Oh wait. I can't run that fast. Charlotte! Dix! Wait! I can't climb this bit. It's too steep. Help me. Help!'

'Reach up. Give me your hand. Careful. Now pull. No, wait Kathryn. I'm slipping. Stop pulling. Stop pulling! Dix! DIX! Help!'

'Honestly, can't you even...? Whoa! Hey, careful. The rock's giving way. Kathryn! Hey! Charlotte! CHARLOTTE!'

'Charlotte?'

'Dix?'

'Are you okay?'

'I think so. Dix... where are we?'

'We're right down on the beach.'

'I feel a bit funny.'

'Me too.'

'The beach looks... different.'

'I've lost my game, Dix.'

'Where's Kathryn?'

'Oh no! We promised her dad.'

'He said he'd come looking if we were late.'

'We'd better find her and get off home.'

'What if she's hurt, Dix? What if she went under those rocks?'

'I dunno. We'll...'

'Look! She's over there. She's okay. Hey. She's got my game. Who's that lot? Kathryn! Who are this lot? Why are you showing them my new game? Give it here.'

'All right. I saved it, didn't I? It could have broken when we fell.'

'Clear off, you lot.'

'Don't, Dix. They're only little kids. They like Charlotte's game. It's magic.'

'Dix, look at the crowds.'

'Why are they in fancy dress? Hey kids, what are you dressed like that for?'

'Yeah, and what are you staring at? Haven't you seen a game before?'

'Go on! Run for your lives. If you *can* run in those old togs. Go on. GERROUT!'

'Go it, Dix. That's sorted them.'

'Come on. Let's go home. I've feel like I've been on this beach for centuries.'

About the Author

Ann is a teacher who has always dabbled in creative writing. She says she spent years wondering whether she was writing stories for children or stories about children, but in the end concluded that it's all too often a false division. As an adult she still enjoys many of the books she read as a youngster, and as a teacher she has been amazed to find her young charges wholly engrossed in books supposedly aimed at people twice and three times their age.

What's That Sniffing at my Window in the Middle of the Night by Rose Thurlbeck

Hey buddy, if you want a story before you go to sleep, you'd better settle down real quick.

Okay then.

One summer not so long ago, the circus came to town. They pitched their camp on Potter's Field as always, and the air was filled with music, the cries of exotic animals and the shouts of the barkers.

That first night the Big Top was packed to the tent pegs and the show was better than ever – the tightrope walkers were more daring, the aerialists flew higher with more twists, the elephants were bigger and the tigers were the fiercest that were ever seen. But almost everyone loved the clowns pretending to be dogs chasing the clowns pretending to be hobos across the sawdust. One of the dogs stole a baby from the audience, setting off a series of events and catastrophes that ended with him standing in triumph atop a plumed white horse, child unharmed, staring at the cheering crowd.

A lot of people walked home happy under the full moon, and a lot of them were looking forward to seeing the show all over again the following evening.

The family who lived in this house before us had a boy who slept in this very room. His name was Daniel and he was wide awake. He didn't like the clowns. When the baby was stolen everyone else was laughing, but Daniel didn't understand that it wasn't a real baby, didn't understand why everyone thought it so funny. He thought it was creepy – especially when the 'dog' was sitting on that huge horse, staring straight at him, smiling.

His mom always told him, 'If something scares you, Chicken, give it a silly name so you can laugh at it.' He tried, but clogs, howns and downs – and you could have *real* nightmares about being chased by a pack of baying downs – was not helping. He re-arranged his bundled blanket and gave himself up to the distraction of night sounds from outside.

The moon shone through the window, casting shadows on the wall, but there was little noise. Oh, sure, he could hear a radio playing from down the street and there was a burst of winged panic rattling against the branches of an old oak. Closer, the bell of a running cat was silenced. There was no wind, but the swing was brushed aside anyway.

Darkness leapt in through the window, landing softly by the bed.

Daniel lay very still with his eyes tight shut, while something – something big – sniffed the air and closed its jaws with a snap. A great weight climbed gently on to the bottom of the bed – like this. Daniel's feet, then his knees, then his thighs were pinned beneath his blanket as the creature stepped slowly and carefully the length of the boy – like this. It stopped, leaning on Daniel's shoulders. His heart beat so hard he thought the house would shake apart – yes, just like this. But Daniel knew as long as his eyes were closed and he kept very still, nothing could hurt him, so he stayed very still. Even when he felt warm breath on his face. Even when he smelled the fur and heard a great tongue rolling over lips and teeth, and a glob of warm drool settled on the end of his chin. Even when his eyes were sniffed and his mouth was snuffled by a cold wet nose. Like this.

Voices. His parents were talking just outside his room. His dad would look in on him! Daniel turned to see light from the hallway shining under the door. *Please,* he screamed silently. *Please look in on me, open the door, I'm not ok, I'm–*

But the door stayed closed, the voices – his mom was laughing – went away and the light went out. Daniel, slowly turned his head, looked up.

The wolf he saw wore a smiling face, a once-human face, a clown's face, and that terrible smile got wider and wider.

Like this.

About the Author

Rose Thurlbeck knows the secret behind a clown's make-up, knows there are no tears behind those dead, staring eyes. Funny, that.

With thanks to Michael Brookes who provided the inspiration for this third story from the Dark Rose garden. It won her the first prize in our horror Fantabble competition.

Good night.

Loft Conversion by Denise Hayes

Kate and Jude's new roof window transformed their shadow-pocked loft into a snug love nest. In candlelight the sloping glass became a black backdrop for reflections of their inverted love making.

Night after night Kate would lie beneath Jude and smile up at her reflection. But one night another girl, sallow faced and hollow eyed, stared back.

Kate screamed and pushed Jude away. The minute she did so, the girl vanished. When Kate tried to explain, Jude was scornful, saying she had simply not recognised her own 'sex face'. Kate knew different. The girl on the roof had lank black hair which even in poor light couldn't be mistaken for Kate's blonde curls.

The next night Kate insisted on making love in darkness. Seeing the figure just in silhouette against the cloudy sky, however, scared her even more.

As the girl only appeared when they made love Kate decided to try a few sexless nights. This got rid of the girl but was not a sustainable solution. So, to avoid looking up at the window, Kate tried different positions during sex. She scissored, she spooned, she went on top. But all the while Kate knew the girl was there and she could feel the burn of her baleful gaze on her skin.

Something had to be done.

In daylight it was easy to see how the girl had got up there. The flat roof of the kitchen side extension provided a stepping stone upwards and the gable end window sill and gothic mouldings were obvious footholds and finger grips. The pitch of the roof was more of a challenge and the drop from the front of the house a little daunting. Kate, however, had a good head for heights.

The girl would be in for a surprise the next time she tried to eavesdrop.

On the Friday night Kate set the trap. She lit scented candles, put romantic music on a loop and dressed in beguiling lacy lingerie. Then she lay on the bed and waited while Jude stripped off.

The lure worked. Kate sensed with a frisson of horrified satisfaction a shifting movement from up above. Bone white fingers lit by the full moon clutched at the window's rim. Kate leapt up and, telling Jude that she'd be back in a tick, headed for the stairs.

She had left a small step ladder in the kitchen which she dragged outside and used to climb on to the extension. The next stage was tricky. She caught the lacy edge of her camisole on the window frame and grazed her elbows and knees as she heaved herself up on to the roof.

She lay for a moment face down and spread-eagled against the cold tiles. Then she lifted her head. The girl was there: a dark outline hunched over the window. Her fingers were splayed against the glass and her face in profile was illuminated in a ghastly chiaroscuro by the flickering light from below.

Given courage by her burning anger Kate inched forwards. She was almost within touching distance of the girl when her foot slipped on a loose tile and with a scream she slithered downwards. Just as Kate approached the roof's edge, the girl turned and looked at her with glittering triumphant eyes.

Kate woke up. She was colder than she'd ever been. She was outside. She was still on the roof, her toes braced against the gutter. It must have somehow halted her fall. There was no sign of the girl. Kate heard noises from the loft; guttural, intense, rhythmic. She crawled upwards.

The view through the window was strange but familiar. There was the bed, its sheets luminous in the candle glow. There was Jude's back, its raven tattoo undulating as if in flight on muscles that rippled with each thrust. And there beneath him was Kate herself, her blonde hair forming Medusa-like tendrils on the silk pillow as she smiled up at the hollow eyed, sallow faced girl on the roof.

About the Author

Denise won second prize in our horror competition with this story. It is one of four stories that were accepted from Denise for inclusion in this anthology.

You will find more of Denise's work in our Sci-Fi anthology Fusion where she was also one of the prize winners.

Denise runs the Twitter project twitter.com/Gregueria1 and blogs on all things creative at;
rosecottagedennysaze.blogspot.co.uk and
dennysaze.blogspot.co.uk.

The Perfect Family by Kester Park

It's a nice room, I reflect for the ten-thousandth time; the cream ceiling and walls in two shades of brown. My children are here; Melissa, Esteban and little Joyce, in their best clothes. We're smiling; at each other, at the walls, at the big dark screen, always smiling.

There are coach-lamps, painted plates, a roaring fireplace. We are happy and nothing ever changes.

This is just one happy time at the end of a long series, though I'd be hard placed to tell you the exact details. One's memory fades as one gets older, wouldn't you say?

If I think really hard, really concentrate – and I tell you, I don't like to – then I can just make out the funniest, faintest memory of darker times; the feeling of being hunted, trapped in a small dark place and never feeling safe.

Sometimes, I ask Melissa or Esteban or even Joyce if they remember but they just smile, or laugh, and say, 'Yes, Mum!' Though sometimes, I catch something in their eyes, that is not a hint of laughter, that is wide and dark and blank, staring out of them, solitary and lost.

But I tell you, we're happy and warm. You see, the fire is roaring quietly in the grate, the tongues of flame captured so picturesquely under the stone mantelpiece.

The dog, Bernard, is lying by Esteban's feet. Dogs always prefer boys, don't you think? At least, that's what my husband used to say. I love my husband, though he's not with us now, not exactly. Sometimes I can feel him, his presence pouring over us like warm custard.

I'm not lonely. I know he loves me better this way, and that's fine. After all, the bad old days; though the memories are as faint as the photocopy of a scan of an old, badly-taken photograph, were pretty bad. All that being scared. Having to wear clothes that covered the bruises. His red face. His body too close. The smell of sweat and spice. Flinching at a sudden movement, and then–

But I'm happy now. I can reach out, put my arm around my children whenever I want. Well, Melissa, anyway. She's the closest. Of course, I can hug the others too. We can all hug each other. I think. We probably do do that; a lot.

'How about a big hug,' I say, suddenly. My children turn their heads to look at me, with eyes like buttons. 'Let's all get up and have a hug,' I cheer. 'Come on, it's hug time!'

'Mum, we can't,' says Melissa.

'What do you mean, we can't? Of course we can!'

She looks agitated. I try to stand up, and the pain fires through me, every nerve and tendon burning. 'Oh my God. What's going on? Why can't I stand?'

I start to beat my fists on the armrests, screaming louder and louder; the children are crying; the dog is snarling.

The noise awakens him. He is quiet for a moment while he registers the source of the cacophony. Then he grunts and rolls out of bed.

I hear the sound of his footsteps coming down the stairs. It's all too familiar, but I can't stop shouting. Hot, jagged words are pouring from me; sparks from a live wire.

He seizes the photograph of his screaming wife and children, and administers three hard blows to the frame with the heel of his hand.

It feels like I've been hit by a tree. By the time my senses report, I am lying, winded on the floor. I hear heaving sobs, see hair collapsed over stricken faces.

Somehow, I get them up, cradle them into their seats; somehow, I compose myself, sit and pose, and smile.

He looks at them. They seem a little tattered and torn but they're smiling the way they should. He feels guilty that they have to live in the photograph but they were unmanageable before. This is a good solution.

Now, they are the perfect family.

About the Author

Kester's story won third prize in our horror competition.

Kester acquired an honours degree in Creative Writing from the University of Hull in 2009.

Thereafter he passed into a phase of extended disorientation, possibly due to a spider bite.

When he became lucid, it was 2014, and he was half way up Mount Pichincha, in Ecuador, swathed in white robes, and faithful acolytes were writing down his every eructation on sacred parchments.

He is very content there as long as the yucca bread isn't too dry and someone wipes away the spittle once in a while.

Entombed by Ulla Susimetsä & Marko Susimetsä

Touching the tomb is forbidden. The excavation will focus on the site around the burial mound, while the tomb itself is protected by the decree of the ethics committee.

Unimaginable stupidity! What good is digging *around* the very place that could give the best clues on the people buried here? This is thought to be the final resting place of a Bronze Age chieftain; a massive pile of stones on a hill, guarded by tall, straight pines. The mighty man has slept here, undisturbed, for centuries. Now he beckons me to reveal his secrets.

I've been here during the day, I know the place, but at night it seems alien. Deserted. Only the moon watches over it now, pouring its light on to the stones, an ethereal silver river. And yet... there is something here, infused into the stones, the earth, the trees and their shadows. Echoes of an ancient grief, perhaps; vows of revenge... they still linger, lie heavy on the mound, an age-old tapestry too intricate for a modern mind to understand.

It resonates with the primitive within, and for a second, the shadowy bond that connects me with the past generations turns into an iron chain.

I place my lantern atop a smooth stone. The candle flame flutters – a small light, barely useful, but slicing this darkness with something more modern would be an act of violence.

I start digging. Careful, one stone at a time.

Something tickles my ear, breathes a whisper into it. I drop a stone from my sweaty hands and reel back, wide-eyed. No one here. Only night and its shadows. I bolster my courage and resume digging.

Then I hear it: a low, fierce murmur, the words just beyond recognition.

My heart hammers, but I must go on. Shivering, I tear into the mound, grasp stone after stone and toss them aside in feverish abandon.

I have that feeling of being watched – as if someone's standing behind me. A cold brush of air on my exposed neck. My imagination leaps to Bronze Age swords and sacrificial blows.

The candle goes out. Fear freezes me, liquefies my bones. There's no wind, not even a breeze. The trees stand still. Nothing moves.

I want to turn and run, but my legs won't move. Only my hands work. I try to stop them, but can't. In the pale moonlight, I watch as they feel for the next mossy stone.

They find nothing. A cold current of air, foetid and foul, springs from the hole in the mound, swirls around me, envelops me.

No moon. No stars. No shadows. Only darkness, still and dense like that squeezed inside a grave. I try to move, but I'm pinioned by the crushing weight of ancient stone above me, all around me.

I scream, but the earth swallows the sound.

I am free! At last, I am free! Fresh night air tastes sweet, the scent of pines is heady, mead-like, after the muddy, stuffy earth and the sharp smell of rocks. I look up; the sky opens wide overhead. I gaze at the stars, the moon... and laugh.

After an eternity in darkness, I have been released. Another took my place and will suffer the torments I endured for so long.

I flex the muscles of the unfamiliar body I tore from my saviour, the offspring of a once great warrior race. What weaklings have they become, how feeble is their will.

I will crush them, drive them before me, revel in the lamentations of their women. This time, no one will stand against me. Grinning, I walk away.

Before me, a wide path slices straight through the forest. Odd; no needles, roots or stones, just a hard, black smoothness. Comfortable to tread, though.

I lift my head. There's a roar ahead, like thunder. And it grows louder fast.

Lights, two blinding bright spots, appear before me. A monster, an immense iron monster, with two shiny eyes. Faster than horses, fast as wind, it–.

About the Authors

Husband and wife team Ulla and Marko are prolific widely published writers. They have been individual prize winners in previous competitions as well as each having authored a story in Elite: Tales from the Frontier.

Learn more about them on the Tales website at www.elite-anthology.co.uk or on Ulla's blog at ususimetsa.blogspot.fi or on Marko's blog at susimetsa.blogspot.fi.

You will also find them on social media:

Ulla: www.facebook.com/ullasusimetsa/ and @ususimetsa

Marko: www.facebook.com/markosusimetsa/ and @msusimetsa

The Sufferers by Jack Mann

Herod stooped outside the cave to examine his map. Rainwater smacked its surface from above, pouring away in all directions. He sheltered it with his body, shook it and studied it again. This was the path Jero had followed, and had Jero seen this cave, he *would* have entered it.

The clouds above were darkening, the worst of the storm yet to come, but there was something about this cave that unsettled Herod, and he wished he could ignore the shelter it offered him. Still, he entered, and activated his lumia crystal at a gentle setting. It would last longer this way, but it would also draw less attention. He did not agree with Jero's suspicions, but felt scorching needles pierce his marrow at the thought there might be truth to them. Though long dead, the legacy of the Sufferers had left an aching scar on the galactic consciousness. Entire cities had committed suicide rather than fall into their hands, while the fates of those captured alive were too hideous to keep records of in archives accessible to the public. A treaty, over a thousand years old, declared the Sufferers a stain upon the fabric of the universe, and one that must be cleansed at any price. It had been signed by every nation in the galaxy.

The cave narrowed further ahead, and then dived too steep to be descended by foot alone. An unpleasant scent fouled the air. Perhaps a dying creature had succumbed in the depths, or a predator had made this its lair. Garglethiders, with their many razor-sharp limbs, were known to snare their prey in the dark recesses of these mountains.

Herod almost turned back, but he knew he would have to return. His chest against the rock, water trickling and dripping on to his face from above, he climbed down until his feet found comfort on the hard rock of the level below. He drew his crystal-fire pistol as he turned, but there was no enemy or creature waiting to strike him. This lower cavity was almost spherical, and in the middle was a still, dark pool. To his left a passage rose up into the rock. Herod followed it.

The smell was getting stronger and his nose wrinkled as he shuffled forward. There was an opening ahead. He pulled himself out into it, froze, and stared.

Arms stretched across a wide, wooden device, a figure in tattered robes sagged over bent knees. Bandages and dressings covered most of the skin that was visible. Cold water dripped from above, soaking the hair of the downcast head.

Herod stepped closer, his voice choked. What remained of the robes were the same as his own. He ran his hand through the sodden hair and pushed it back to see better the face beneath.

Jero's left eye remained closed. His right eye was gone; a charred opening gaped from where it had once been. His nose had been cut so that over half of it was missing, the mucosal lining within exposed. As Herod wondered whether Jero still lived, his master opened his near-toothless mouth to breathe, producing the foul breath of one who has been starved for many days.

'Jero,' Herod pleaded, 'what have they done to you?'

Jero opened his one remaining eye. It was shot red with blood in every part of it that once was white.

'Jero!' Herod squeezed Jero's shoulders.

Jero blinked, a weary movement without hope or gratitude, and then opened his mouth, releasing the stench of his unfed stomach once more, 'Kill me before ... they come ... back.'

Herod turned. Footsteps were approaching.

Jero's eye stared into Herod's as he tried, but failed, to speak again.

Herod fired the pistol into Jero's charred eye-socket. His friend's body sagged, lifeless. The sound of unfamiliar tongues, calling to one another, grew louder, and filled Herod's heart with ice. Trembling, he put the muzzle of the gun to his own temple. He hoped the weapon had sufficient charge left.

About the Author

Jack is a Medical Doctor and Consultant Dermatologist working in the UK. He feels honoured to have had his work included in the fantabble horror anthology, and be named among so many accomplished writers. Prior to this he has published in the medical scientific literature.

Jack has been determined to write science fiction since he was in primary school. The universe in which *The Sufferers* is set is also the setting for a completed full length novel he has written, and at least four sequels he is planning.

A Perfect Match by Denise Hayes

I can't get the child to stand up. I've created the perfect place to put her - a narrow hollowed-out cavity in the wood - but every time I try to stand her there she falls over. Having read advice from fellow enthusiasts on the web I've decided against superglue: apparently it sticks fine - so much so that the soles of the shoes often stay put but the legs break and you're left with two amputated feet but nothing else.

I have had no such problems with the railway figures from my usual suppliers. They come attached to almost invisible squares of sticky plastic. But it's getting harder and harder to find suitable children so I've had to look further afield. I need to get a perfect match, you see.

Apart from the standing-up problem, my tin box diorama is almost finished. I've used a Hills Junior Balsam cough-drops container and put a spooky picture of a rickety helter skelter on the inside of the lid. In the main part of the tin I have placed a wooden insert which contains several carved recesses. In the top right space is a policeman – looking the wrong way of course (my private joke). In the bottom left recess is my balloon seller, gaudily dressed and holding aloft a host of lurid balloons. The little girl is to go into a tiny space in the bottom right corner. I think I'll make her face the wall as if in punishment. That'll look more sinister and get over the problem of mismatched features. Not that there's too much detail at a scale of 1:76 but – as you've probably guessed – I'm a perfectionist. The real girl had a fringe and freckles not a central parting and unblemished skin.

I know what you're thinking: why not buy unpainted figures and customise them myself? I've considered that. I quite like the white and ghostly look of the unadulterated little children. But it's still hard to get the right hairstyle and the correct age group and so on. Besides, I've thought of a better option. One that will help me to focus and select.

I'll probably have to source my subjects in a different type of place. After the last two children some parents are getting a bit more protective – especially at fairgrounds. But not all. From where I'm standing, just beside the carousel, I can see at least three possibilities. I look again at the children in the palm of my hand. One – a little girl – is just a bit taller than a toddler and has blond plaits and a dress well above her knees. And here she is: bored with waiting for her siblings to come from the ride, wandering away from her distracted father who's taking pictures of his two remaining children. They wave from their perches on the bobbing painted horses. I've always thought that carousel horses are a bit unsettling – such staring eyes and fierce flaring nostrils. That has given me an idea for the image in my new tin. It's all a work in progress, you know.

The little girl is coming towards me, fiddling with her hair and singing to herself. As she passes by I hand her a red balloon. I'm only holding one of course – more would make me too memorable. Sometimes accuracy has to be sacrificed for safety. 'Hello, little girl,' I whisper in her ear, 'I've lost my favourite balloon. It's shaped like a duck and you can have it if you help me find it.' She glances at her father but – like the others – she's greedy and stupid. She nods and takes my hand.

So there you are. Problem solved. Now I've reversed the selection process I can keep on buying the easy-to-stand figures. As for the girl in the helter skelter diorama, I simply glued the whole front of her body to the back wall of the tin. She's never turning round again. No one will ever see her face.

About the Author

This is the third of four stories written by Denise that appear in this anthology.

Denise runs the Twitter project twitter.com/Greguerial and blogs on all things creative at;

rosecottagedennysaze.blogspot.co.uk and

dennysaze.blogspot.co.uk.

I hold still, wooden stake in hand, and can only hope the shadow will conceal me.

How did I get talked into this? I'm trained. I'll be laughed out of the precinct if anyone finds out.

It began with an argument in a bar.

'There's no such thing as ghosts!' I'd had a few and was laying down the law. Up to our eyes in real evil, tracking killers and all this lot had to worry about were disembodied voices.

One of the women melted out of the conversation once it became animated, but kept shooting me glances when she thought I wasn't looking.

No surprise when she sidled up after the noise and bustle had moved on. Her little boy had heard the voices too. They wanted her to get a psychic in. What did I think?

'There'll be a rational explanation,' I told her. 'There always is.'

'Please come and look.'

It was a neat apartment.

'Real voices,' her boy told me. 'Soft. Scary. I can't hear words.'

I smiled. 'An echo, for sure. It's a big old place.'

The caretaker was knocking ninety but he pulled out the building plans for me.

I was on my own in the boy's room wondering about maintenance ducts when out of nowhere a voice spoke. Low, no distinguishable words, yet it sent a shiver through me.

'Kids in the basement. We'll go tomorrow. Catch them at it.'

What I found the next evening was the whole ghost-hunting group. 'You can't come,' they told me. 'We can't have a sceptic at the heart of it.'

They reckoned they were the trained ones with their incense. OK, I thought, chanting nutters waving candles are as likely as anyone to scare the pants off a bunch of kids. I smiled inwardly. 'I'll wait here. Tread softly.'

Incense is one thing, but then I saw a wooden stake brandished. 'I'll keep that.'

And that's how I've ended up here holding the thing like some credulous pagan as their footsteps whisper away, overlain by the low hum of their chanting, into the dark of the maintenance duct. I ease back into the shadow.

If they could have five minutes facing the evil I've had to face in my line of work, they'd snuff out their scented candles in a trice.

The reverberation of the old ducting lets me follow their progress as background to my thoughts.

I'm angry that I shivered at an echo up in the apartment. My investigator's instinct should stop me jumping at shadows.

Nothing but the day job should make me shiver. Like listening to the recordings of the killers we're tracking but have yet to catch. The thought of those *real* voices stands up the hairs at the back of my neck.

I've forgotten the chant but my head snaps up when it stops. A sudden cut. A shriek of pure terror whistles down the ducting to where I stand. Then silence.

What the hell?

I'm alert, every sense tingling. The silence breaks in the crash of running footsteps – rhythmic, deliberate – coming closer. It wasn't a ghost my instincts jumped at. Of course it wasn't. I don't believe in ghosts. My subconscious recognised the resonance of the voice. The tapes. The killings. The horrors that we've been drowning in for weeks. I've stumbled into the heart of it. Where better to hide than the bowels of a huge apartment block with an ancient caretaker and access to the city streets through drains and access shafts?

I've found them! It's the breakthrough we've prayed for. And now the killers have silenced the ghost-hunters, they're leaving their lair to check their hidden entrances, to see who else has unearthed their secret. I can't run, not with the way sound echoes through this place. I have no weapon but the one I already hold, no place to hide in this bare-walled underground world.

I hold still, wooden stake in hand, and can only hope the shadow will conceal me.

About the Author

JX dabbles equally in music and words and considers himself to be a more accomplished wordsmith than musician. He has insisted on being known by his initials (JX – JayEx) since he was four.

The number of the beast by Celia Coyne

We all have a number. Me? I'm one in a hundred, according to psychologists. Those who are born like me have a capacity for extreme violence without conscience. Of course, you can't tell who I am just by looking at me. I walk unnoticed among all the other statistics: the seven in 100,000 who will suffer a brain tumour, the eight people who will drown in a garden pond this year.

Who shall I be for you? The Grim Reaper, Kali, the Devil? I like to think I'm just a person doing what I was born to do. I know my purpose; there's not many who can say that. I like to think that I do my job well.

These Auckland summers are something else when the weather is so warm and close, the air just hanging there, making people sticky. That's how it is this morning. I checked the forecast – there's an 80 per cent chance of a storm. When it's so hot and humid, people sleep with their windows open. Even though they heard about me on the evening news; even though they know I strike at night. They take their chances. After all, the risk of being murdered is one in 100,000. It always happens to someone else, right?

I've parked my car on the edge of the estate. It's 4am. As I walk down the street I see someone walking towards me. My heart sinks as it means I'll probably have to turn back - take a day off, so to speak. But as I move closer I see that it's a man in pyjamas. He's looking straight at me but he's somewhere else – a sleepwalker going for a stroll. I wonder where he'll end up. Will he cross the motorway and cause a pile up? Will he wake up in the middle of a field?

I let him pass by and I look at the brooding sky. The street is quiet and empty; this is my domain, a hunting ground. But who will it be? I look for open windows; I don't like to force my way in. The window I choose is on the side of the house, partially hidden by a tall gate. I look into the room. A woman is sleeping in a bed. In her restless sleep, she has thrown the single sheet half off her body. Then I'm in the room. I move silently, checking the rest of the house, looking for the vigilant red eyes of burglar alarms. There are none and I note that two people are asleep in the next room.

Most people die in their own homes, mainly by falling down the stairs. If people only knew how dangerous stairs are. Most murders happen here, too, the majority of them in the kitchen. Think of all those handy household implements: the kitchen knives, the irons, the frying pans. Most people are murdered by someone they know.

But what are the chances of being murdered in your bed by a stranger? There's a number for that if you dig deep enough.

Firm pressure on the carotid arteries – it doesn't take a lot of force. Unconsciousness followed by death. The house is quieter without the sound of her breathing. Now, like the others, she has a number that only *I* know.

I let myself out through the front door. Then I'm walking back to the car and the sky is lightening. The storm has moved on and will empty its rain on some other town.

When I get to the car I take off my gloves and coveralls. Then I look at the map – it takes a lot of preparation to be convincingly random. I've got a 200-mile drive ahead. I have to keep one step ahead all the time if I am to keep doing my job.

You're asking me why I do it. But that's a bit like asking why the earth keeps orbiting the sun. It just does. It's an odds-on certainty.

About the Author

Celia was highly commended by the judges in our horror competition for this story. Celia comes with an impressive writing track record having worked in publishing for twenty years, as a journalist and editor of non-fiction. In her fiction writing she enjoys exploring unusual themes and ideas.

His Spectre by John D Scotcher

He checks in at seven. Hollow chimes of a grandfather clock in the hotel restaurant sound his arrival like a requiem bell.

'Will you be with us more than one night, sir?'

He shakes his head. 'Just the one.' His voice, thick with regret. Always just the one.

He eats alone in the crowded restaurant. A fat American tourist whispers to her sister. 'Oh Maud! That guy. He might be the loneliest person I have ever seen. Let's ask him to join us.'

As if he hears, he latches on to her gaze with sunken, haunted eyes. She turns away with a shudder. She doesn't look back.

The restaurant thins out. He's in no rush to leave. Not sober. 'Brandy.' He motions to the waitress. 'The bottle.' She rushes away, glad to be free from his funereal stare.

His great love lasted a summer. He'd wanted it to last forever. An affair in the oldest sense of the word. Chance meeting, blossoming love, the fantasy of future plans, then reality, ending and regret. Emily had wanted to leave Olly, but finally children and family had forced her hand. She'd told him, 'If things were different. If only I wasn't with him.'

The waitress sets down the brandy and scuttles away. He lifts the bottle, then turns it in his hand before he pours. The same hand. The hand that killed.

Killing, it turned out, had been easy. He'd considered it a crime of passion, but he'd planned it with ice cold precision. Olly liked a fast car and drove it like a fool. Olly knew the country roads by his home. Olly never expected an obstacle to be placed in his path.

By the third glass of brandy he is alone. The other guests have moved to the bar. The waitress is gone, hesitating to ask him to move. The buzz of alcohol blossoms in his blood, but he still feels the temperature plummet. He's been expecting it. He expects it every night. Yet still its arrival chills his soul, kills his hope. He has been found. It will not be long now.

He'd never believed in ghosts. He'd never believed in much of anything except himself and his ability to guide the world to his own hand. He'd driven past the twisted wreck of Olly's car and smiled, thinking, 'I could probably stop. He's possibly still alive right now.' Then he'd driven on. No one else would be along that country lane until it was too late.

The candles flicker in the restaurant. He glances up. Soon.

In the bar, guests pull clothes tighter to their necks against the sudden chill. In ones or twos, they slink away to their rooms, shooting distrustful looks at faces they were laughing with but a moment before. In the kitchen, the chef pulls on his coat and steals into the night, dirty dishes discarded by the sink. At reception the manager pops up the 'ring for service' sign early and escapes to the warm safety of his room. Someone switches off the lobby light.

He sits in the darkness and waits.

There is an almost imperceptible shimmer in the air. The grandfather clock ticks the last moments to the inevitable. Then it is there.

A tear comes to his eye at the sight of it. Killing had turned out to be easy. Killing the right person had turned out to be hard. He shifts in his seat, turning to face the spectre, waiting for it to start forward towards him. As it always does.

He wanted to spend every night of his life with her. He's succeeded. She will follow him until he dies. She draws near, then lifts her face to him. Lips part in a ghastly smile of recognition. Dead eyes reflect all he has done to her, her motherless children, the void where she lived.

He smiles through his tears. Her presence makes him lonelier than he had ever imagined.

'Hello my love,' he whispers.

About the Author

John is an invited contributor to this anthology. He was born in 1970 in Taplow, just outside London. He grew up in Maidenhead, Berkshire and spent much of his youth on the Thames where his novel *The Boy In Winter's Grasp* is set.

He has had many jobs including teacher, graphic designer, tie-designer and assistant film director. He now lives in Northampton where he splits his time between running his web development business and writing.

Assisted by Richard Dixon

It was early, the sun not yet risen when Mary picked up the note from the oak kitchen table. A single candle, attached to a saucer by virtue of its substantially melted wax was sitting beside it as it had been when she had finally ascended to her room the previous evening. The nights were long and cold and she cloaked herself in her khaki padded jacket, taking it from its peg beside the cellar door which she opened.

Dearest Mary,

I know that when I rise again I will be in tremendous pain but that the end will come expeditiously thereafter. Whilst I firmly believe that this is not what you truly want, we both know that it is right.

After all we discussed yesterday evening, I promised you I would not drink last night and here I am returned at nearly 3 am. Forgive me. It was, after all, my last.

It was good to spend time together again and to converse without the anguish and anger, on either of our parts I believe, as the husband and wife we purport to be. Perhaps I should have been more open with you.

Even as I write that, I know I should. My history should never have been something to cause you distress but something I would like to think even now you could have embraced. Perhaps I was selfish, maybe I should have gone after you when you left but my love for you and my desire not to lose our special relationship prevented me.

I have been so lucky to have had you. Your family were there when I was first weak and needed someone. I know how much you must have loved them and must privately miss them now; I hope that in my own way I have been able to be a comfort to you.

We have had some wonderful times, you and I, at least in those early days. The view of Paris at night, candlelit dinner on the Seine and you there to look after my needs. That has remained a cherished memory for me.

You have protected me for so long, made me comfortable and sheltered me when I have been vulnerable and for this I cannot thank you enough. Inevitably, the strain was always going to take its toll; I was always going to become a burden. I do not blame you for the times you left me, abandoned me, and I know that on more than one occasion I have crossed the line and put you in a difficult, no, impossible, position.

In recent years it has grown so much harder for me to find the means to keep up my strength and should you find me revitalised I know that only causes you further sadness. Bind yourself in neither guilt nor shame after I am gone, such clothes are not yours to bear, let me take them with me.

As agreed, to confirm my commitment to this conclusion, I have placed the necessary instruments so you will find them beside me in the morning. I beseech you to stick to your part of our arrangement. I trust you will have slept well tonight for you will need all your strength with you when you come to me. If you should falter, I believe you will fail yourself and in time, regrettably, no doubt others.

I am tired and have grown weary and I am ready to rest again now.

The earth feels comfortable, as always but also tonight, inviting, as though it knows.

My undying love,

Gregor

Having made her way down to the cellar, Mary crumpled the letter, tossing it onto the spilt earth and wiping a tear on her jacket sleeve. She rested one hand on the cold aged lid for a moment, head bowed, murmuring the Lord's Prayer, praying for the strength to see her long-overdue actions through. Steadying her nerves, she pushed aside the lid and reached for hammer and wood.

About the Author

Richard Dixon was born in 1966 in Grimsby and holds a PhD and degree in Mathematics and Computing from the University of Hull. Having spent many years in the field of Health Informatics he currently works in traffic-related software design. Although having had an interest in writing and horror in particular since school, it is only recently, after a number of competition successes, that Richard has added short-story writing to his range of hobbies which also includes cryptic crosswords and railways. Richard is currently helping to recreate a part of history as a director at the Yorkshire Wolds Railway in East Yorkshire.

Learn more at: www.yorkshirewoldsrailway.org.uk

The Statue in the Playground by Darren Grey

'I think it's a Viking god,' said Roger, who always liked to get his opinion in first.

The children stood round the tall, wooden statue of a man. This new addition to the park had attracted their attention immediately upon their arrival. Its carven features stared down at them with intensity, its sombre eyes set above a ruddy face and a short beard. Its mouth hung open as if on the cusp of speaking.

'Do you think it's magic?' asked Billy, his neck bent backwards as he looked straight up at the towering figure.

'No, I doubt that,' replied Roger, authority rising in his voice. 'It's probably some god that's dead by now. Maybe from Iceland or Scandavialand. Somewhere like that. They have lots of old gods there but no one prays to them anymore, so they've all died off. Even if it had magic in it there probably wouldn't be very much left now that it's been put here.'

The children crowded closer round the statue, trying to detect some ancient divine energy from the dark wood or some god-like expression in the detailed lines of the statue's face. The statue continued to stare down at them in solemn silence. When no evidence of miracles immediately presented itself their minds began to wander again.

'His eyes look sad,' said Billy, continuing to analyse the statue's face. 'Why do you think they made his eyes so sad?' No one responded.

'My dad says it's out of a movie, one with dragons and things in it,' said Jessika, twisting a pigtail around her finger. The rest of the group ignored her. They'd learned long ago that any statement beginning with 'My dad says' meant it was likely made up on the spot.

'It's probably just one of a thousand statues made in a factory somewhere,' said Victoria, crossing her arms. 'There's really nothing special about it. I don't know why you're making such a fuss. You're all so childish sometimes.' Her dismissive attitude broke the spell around the group, and the statue became just a normal object, devoid of mystery.

Victoria walked up to the statue and knocked on the dark wood. 'See? It's hollow. Probably isn't even real wood. It was just made in some big factory out of plastic stuff and empty inside. I bet there's loads just the same, all empty.'

The hot sunshine beat down on the children as they shuffled round the statue. There seemed nothing further that could be said about this new attraction, yet they found it hard to put aside their curiosity.

'It's not empty,' said Celia in a low voice. The children all turned to her – it wasn't like Celia to say something without being prompted first.

'There's a man in there,' she continued, staring down at the statue's feet as she talked. 'He tried to hurt me, here in the park. It was yesterday evening and I was all alone. He put his hand over my mouth and I couldn't cry out. So I trapped him. I trapped him in wood. He can't get out now.'

The children exchanged glances, a cold silence settling over them.

'Let's go and play on the swings,' said Roger, pushing Celia's comments out of his mind. The children all ran off, shouting at each other as they went, leaving Celia behind.

The young girl took soft steps towards to the statue and reached her hand up to its chest. She turned her small face to look up into the sad wooden eyes.

'I can hear you screaming still,' she said. 'No one else can, but I hear, and I know. You'll be screaming for a long long time. I'll come visit you every day just to hear you scream.'

She turned and skipped off to join the others, her laughter joining their shouts and cries, loud and free in the sunshine. The statue stared on sadly, its fixed eyes unable to look away. Inside, deep down, a man screamed in silence.

About the Author

Darren is a prolific science fiction and fantasy author, originally from Dublin, who these days lives in London, working in project management in scientific research. Darren grew up with a mix of Tolkien, astronomy and computer games injecting a love for imagination into his meat-based brain. As well as creative writing he makes his own computer games at GamesofGrey.com.

Darren's work also appears in Elite: Tales from the Frontier.

Find Darren on Twitter at @dgrey0

The In-terror-gator by Isla Sandford Hall

He sat on the edge of the chair apprehensively, as if he was going to jump up at any moment. He swallowed. He could hear a slight scraping noise coming from the direction of the two-way mirror opposite. He felt scrutiny from behind it dripping off the walls of the small bare room, despite the fact that the suspect couldn't see him. The only other pieces of furniture were a couple of uncomfortable metal chairs and a cold steel table with two sets of handcuffs attached to it. Neither cuffed him. It was his first interrogation.

Someone screamed. 'What are you doing? GET AWAY! HELP! PLEASE! HELP!'

The first body was strewn across the warehouse, its leaking blood dyeing the walls and floor a bright unforgivable red. The head was hanging off the old disused hat stand, alongside a mismatched pair of gloves and a faded velvet frockcoat. One foot was dangling from the bare light-bulb by a string of tendon; its counterpart lying forgotten by the door, as if it had been trying to escape without its body. The torso (most of it) was caught in the

rubbish chute, a strand of broken intestine the only thing fastening it to the gruesome scene.

'Where were you at four thirty yesterday afternoon?'

'The grocery store.'

'Alone?'

'With my mother.'

'I heard she lived in Canada?'

'She moved.'

'How long ago? Remind me of her maiden name.'

'Why? Do my mother's affairs affect you?'

'You've heard about the disappearances? We suspect foul play.'

'I don't see what that has to do with me.'

He jumped when the door opened, letting a bright light stream into the small space. The steel table reflected the glow harshly, and he closed his eyes for a second to adjust to the change. He glanced at the person who had appeared in the door frame, staring at him. A person of average height, with one of those faces, and holding a knife. Some loony; the boys would deal with it. He turned back to the mirror to wrap up the investigation.

The pub was crowded.

'Did you hear about the latest murder?'

'Yeah, the boy who was killed lived on my block. The police were up and down all day questioning people.'

'Find anything?'

'Don't think so ...'

'Oh well ... s'pose it can't be helped.'

She was in a bar, half out of her mind with drink. When the man came, she welcomed the chance for a quick fling, or maybe a few more beers on him. She never expected him to be ... well, that.

The second and third bodies were mixed in among the remains of a 'killer' party. A scrambled mess of plastic cups, alcohol-induced vomit and still-fresh body parts. One was a girl, the other too mangled to recognise.

'I have reason to suspect you of the murders of–'

'You have no right!'

'I'm acting on behalf of the law. Of course I have a right!'

'I want a lawyer.'

The fourth body was mostly intact, apart from random holes dotting its torso. It was in the penguin enclosure at the zoo, and was found by a new employee who – over the span of a few hours – fainted, resigned and arranged to move to a safer (though pricier) neighbourhood. Only then did he go to the police. By the time they could get a pathologist to analyse the body, it was too late; there was nothing to learn.

Silence.

The fifth was only discovered when the street-lamps were lit, the shadows of her dangling heels dancing on the pavement.

'You still there, sir? I said I want a lawyer. Are you there?'

Number six was perhaps the worst of all. The first officer went white; the second puked, the third fainted and the fourth had to be led outside shaking.

Silence.

They found the seventh victim, but they never found his body.

About the Author

Isla Sandford Hall was born in 2002. She lives in London with her family and six cats. A Hebridean childhood without cars, electricity or hot water has inspired an ambition to live on the wild island of Gometra and write. Her favourite colours are black and purple and she was once described as a goth by an art teacher, suggesting her suitability for the horror genre. Her school doesn't believe in exams, but if it did she would have multiple academic qualifications with which to reach this ambitious word count. An amateur violinist, blacksmith and backgammon player; she is an avid reader, country murder ballad enthusiast and proud Ravenclaw presently working on her first novel.

Facing Up by Richard Dixon

For the last few days she had felt more emotions than she could ever have conceived existed and ever-present through all of them had been the pain, the perpetual reminder of the nightmare situation in which Cassie found herself.

She stood with her back against the wall, knees bent, her head back, bathing in the comforting warmth from the slowly dying log fire. The latter provided the only illumination in the stark, begrimed room of the somewhat dilapidated cottage her sister had agreed to let her occupy, provided she promised not to leave anything unsavoury or illegal lying around. And Christ alone knew she needed something.

The flickering light played across her closed eyelids as she steeled herself for what was to come. There were no guidebooks for this but Cassie had made her decision.

Although it felt like an eternity had passed, she had been there at most half an hour, waiting, coping. She could sense it had entered, or rather arrived, and summoned the courage to open her eyes.

The fire, reduced to a single glowing log, mustered the energy for one last Danse Macabre. And there it was, the horror of its shape softened by the dim light, slightly indistinct as though some small part existed in a dimension she was not designed to register, eyes of mahogany piercing her own as it had the first time, reaching into her soul, reading her most precious thoughts.

The beguiling demonic creature tilted its horned head a few degrees towards one shoulder, perhaps finding a better angle for its visual incision. Cassie winced and in spite of her intention was forced to allow her laboured exhalation to carry an anguished cry.

It elongated its mandible giving its dark hollow mouth a Munchian expression. Cassie tried to focus her thoughts on what it might do next, whilst allowing the subconscious part of her to concentrate on managing the agony her body was enduring.

She blinked momentarily and found the hideous visage barely an inch in front of hers without it seemingly having moved. Its breath enveloped her face like the heat from an opened oven and she tried in vain to recoil from it, blocked by the harsh yet reassuring reality of the room wall.

Her heart should have been in overdrive but it was remarkably calm, idling – she could hear the steady pulse inside her head as she stared into those rich menacing, yet alluring eyes trying not to think of the stiletto finger that was now firmly pressed against her abdomen. Cassie tensed in anticipation of what the creature might have in mind for her.

The long black nail scratched through her pitifully delicate top and she could feel its smooth subtle blade drawing downwards. The sensation was of it penetrating deep into her flesh yet it had barely cut the skin. Cassie shuddered involuntarily as it continued on its surgical journey.

The creature removed its digit and, placing it prominently between their faces, licked at the blood. They stared at one another until, as unperceived as it had approached, the creature had withdrawn and stood there naked, at once dreadful and enticing, its foreboding leathery hide glistening in the half-light afforded by the fading embers.

And it laughed - one single, hollow, callous laugh – then, retracting its jaw, turned its back and started to move away, curiosity satiated. Its shape began to lose its stability once more as it did so, bound for the Hellish dimension in which it surely dwelt.

The searing pain returned to Cassie and, released from the captivating aura of the demon's gaze, she bent and clutched her stomach, feeling the rivulets of dark bubbling blood that stained her ripped top and dripped to the floor.

Fighting back the hurt, Cassie raised her head and stared after the departing form.

'Don't you dare go!' she screamed.

The creature paused, half turning its blurred head towards her.

'This,' she cried, pointing to her rounded bloodied belly, 'is your responsibility, too!'

About the Author

This is the second of two stories by Richard in this anthology.

Parents' Evening by CM Angus

Bryan looked from me to Claire and back again. 'He's got it in for me, Dad,' he said. 'He keeps saying it's me, but it's not. It's Josh.'

Josh was one of the other boys in Bryan's class.

'I'm not lying, Dad,' he insisted.

Last week had been tough. Parents' evening had come and Mr Calder's assessment of Bryan had been less than stellar. 'He needs to take responsibility for his actions and stop playing the fool,' he'd said, 'and this nonsense about Josh has to stop.'

'Josh does it and I get the blame,' Bryan had said on the verge of tears. 'It's always the same. It's Josh, Dad, not me, but Mr Calder won't listen. What he does is wrong. He scares me, Dad.'

Bryan wouldn't back down and, in an attempt to clear the air, we invited Mr Calder to dinner. Bryan had been seriously displeased, especially with Claire whose idea it had been.

'I'm your mum, Bryan,' Claire had said to him. 'You need to learn when it's time to back down. We're going to relax over a nice meal and then discuss this all together.'

On the stroke of seven, Mr Calder arrived wearing jeans, a Harris Tweed jacket and carrying a bottle of wine.

'Pass the mashed potatoes to Mr Calder, Bryan,' Claire said.

We were sitting in the kitchen, but Bryan seemed frozen in his seat. That wasn't like him. It was as though he was afraid.

'It's OK, I can reach,' Mr Calder said. 'Can I offer you some more wine?'

We'd agreed that we'd have dinner first and then talk. The meal continued, but there wasn't much relaxation with Bryan monosyllabic and scowling. We adults ended up drinking a little too much, and a little too quickly. As we finished dessert, I could see Claire looked fraught and Bryan hadn't lost his stony glare.

Excusing myself, I went upstairs to the bathroom.

A sudden commotion. A crash of plates. A scream...

Then silence.

Even as I scrambled to pull up my zip, I heard hammering, saw the handle twist.

'Dad! Help!' It was Bryan, his voice desperate as he clawed at the door.

Wrenching it open I swept the distressed child into my arms and ran downstairs.

A banging noise sounded from outside, like repeated attempts to kick in the door.

'Dad! He did it. He did it to Mum.'

He scares me, Bryan had said. I'd assumed he'd meant Josh.

Slumped over the blood-soaked dinner table was Claire, head to one side, dead eyes staring out at nothing. I could see her throat had been cut and in the middle of her back, our large chef's knife had been thrust, handle now pointing at the ceiling.

There was nothing I could do for her, but I must save Bryan. Dropping him, I grabbed the phone and another knife and edged out of the kitchen, hurrying him ahead of me.

The desperate banging still sounded. Somehow Bryan had locked him out but he was determined.

Bryan had warned us something was wrong. Why hadn't we listened? No wonder he'd looked scared.

'It was him, Dad,' Bryan gasped through sobs. 'He killed Mum. It was horrible.' He tore frantically at his hair. 'It's my fault; he wouldn't be here if I hadn't...'

'Hold this.' I handed Bryan the knife as I dialled the police.

'Yes... my son's teacher... murdered my wife ... He's locked out but ... I don't know... please hurry.'

'Come on Bryan.'

We barricaded ourselves in the bathroom.

'*He* did it, Dad,' wailed Bryan. 'But why?'

'I don't know, Bryan; I don't know why Mr Calder did it.'

'Not Mr Calder, Josh.'

'No, Bryan, Josh isn't...'

'He's always here, Dad.'

'It's OK, Bryan, give me the...'

Heaviness filled my chest... more warmth than pain. I looked down at the knife now lodged in my side. An involuntary cough spattered bright blood up the wall.

'Bryan?'

'Bryan isn't here any more ... Call me Josh.'

About the Author

CM Angus grew up in the North East of England and now lives in Yorkshire with his wife and children. He is interested in all things creative and technological.

Having previously published technical non-fiction, he is currently working on his first novel under the working title Fixpoint - a speculative-fiction spanning three generations of one family haunted by an approaching alternate-reality where their children have been erased from history.

Follow his writing on his blog at cmangus.blogspot.co.uk

Can This Day Possibly Get any Worse? by Regina Puckett

Shirley scrambled out of bed and ran into the bathroom. She stayed in the shower only long enough to shampoo her hair. She tried drying it but the hair dryer wouldn't work. Throwing it into the sink, she ran a comb through her hair. In quick succession, she ruined three pairs of panty hose, popped two buttons off her favorite white blouse, broke the heel off her only pair of high heels and spilled coffee on her one remaining clean dress. Over an hour late and frustrated, she screamed, 'Can this day get any worse?'

She blamed the abysmal beginning to her morning on her next door neighbors. Because of them, she'd had to take a sleeping pill the night before to block out the hectic activity of blue lights and high-pitched screaming. Even after living next to them for three years, she couldn't get used to their mega fights or them calling the police on each other.

Finally dressed, Shirley ran out the front door and plowed face-first into a firm chest. When she looked up, a stern policeman stared down at her as if she might be an escaped mental patient.

She took a step back. 'I'm sorry.' He turned his attention to the large coffee stain on her dress which she covered with her hand. 'Is there something I can help you with?

He nodded toward her neighbor's house. 'We're conducting a house to house, looking for the Henry's youngest daughter. She's been missing since late yesterday afternoon.'

She let him in. While he searched her house, she again wondered how many things could possibly go wrong in one day.

It wasn't until he had completed his search that it occurred to her that the Henry's were having a worse day.

'Is there anything I can do to help? That poor child. What could have happened to her?'

He paused before saying, 'Mr. Henry is out helping in the search but Mrs. Henry is at home. She's been crying uncontrollably all night. Maybe there's something you can do to comfort her.'

After three long hours of listening to Marie wail and sniffle, Shirley volunteered to go out for coffee and snacks for the volunteers and family. She had to take Marie's rusted old 1995 Cadillac Eldorado instead of her own because some of the volunteers' and police cars had blocked her driveway.

On the long drive back to the Henry's house, the smell of the fresh donuts was a distracting reminder that she had missed out on breakfast. Just as she reached over to grab one, there was a loud bang and the car slid off the road and into a ditch. Dazed by the rapid turn of events, she turned off the car and laid her forehead on the steering wheel. 'Seriously? What else can possibly go wrong today?' Without another car in sight, she got out and walked around the Henry's to see what had happened. The driver's rear tire was shredded to pieces. She knew nothing about changing tires.

Shirley decided she might as well eat a donut while waiting for someone to come by and stop to offer help. She was just settling to do that when another car pulled in behind the Henry's. Something was finally going her way.

A young officer climbed out and touched the brim of his hat. 'Looks like you need help, ma'am. Pop the trunk.'

'Thank you.' She reached inside the driver's window and pulled the release. When she turned to join him, she stopped in mid-step, facing a levelled gun.

'Seriously?'

He nodded toward the trunk. 'There's a dead child in there.'

Of course there was, because that was just the way her day was working out. She opened her mouth to say she had no idea how it had got there when a car came out of nowhere and struck the police officer. He went flying through the air and landed in the ditch.

'Can this day possibly get any worse?'

About the Author

Regina is an invited contributor to this anthology. She is a 2014 Readers' Favorite Award winning author for her sweet romance, *Concealed in My Heart*. Her steampunk book, *I Will Breathe*, and her children's picture book, *Borrowed Wings*, both received the Children's Literary Classic Seal of Approval. *I Will Breathe* was selected as a Science Fiction Finalist in the 2015 IAN Book of the Year Awards. Her boxed set, *A TOUCH OF PASSION*, is the 2016 winner of the Romance Reviews Readers' Choice Awards.

She writes sweet romances, horror, inspirational, steampunk, picture books and poetry. There are always several projects in various stages of completion and characters and stories waiting in the wings for their chance to finally get out of her head and onto paper.

Opening doors by Penny Grubb

Fire sparkled in flickers of memory, pushing open doors with its roaring flame. A shower of sticks falling, gaudy red ends like candy. Sharp to the taste.

'Chris'sakes! Look at the mess. I've told you not to leave matches out.'

'He shouldn't fecking touch what's not fecking his.'

'Give over. He's only a babby.'

'I'll teach him. Come here, Gav.'

An eruption of eye-searing white burst from the sharp-tasting candy, trailing tendrils of reds and yellows. Reaching out to touch... a knife-blade of pain sears through his hand.

Shouts and screams.

'What've you done to him, bastard!'

'He'll not go near matches again.'

'I'll have to keep him off the childminder, now. Gav, shurrup that screaming. You're doing my head in.'

His hand healed, but the power of the flame scarred his soul.

Late one night after the noise had quietened to laboured breathing and rattly snores he crept out looking for food. He found bread, greenish and funny tasting, and a fat box of matches.

He lit them one by one as he wandered round, thirsty, looking for milk. Tiny fires flared. The bottle was heavy, tasted bad. He let it fall. Iridescent liquid trickled across the floor, lapped at one of the miniature fires. It swooshed high in a great sweep of flame.

Power!

Screams. Others, not him this time.

The door opened on a new life. New adults. Always in his face. Kinda nice at first. Biscuits, milk, warmth. But no matches and he needed fire.

'Odd little tyke. Always scratting in corners for something.'

Then he found a single match in a groove of the floor. No liquid for power, but curtains worked well enough.

The new door opened on a place with more children and fewer adults, one of them called Sir, who made him do things. He found another match, put it to Sir's bed one night. That was the end of that.

The next door opened on a place with locked doors, bars at the windows. Two guys set a match to a pile of torn sheets, flapping and blowing to nurture the tiny spark. Anger bubbled over as he stamped contemptuously on their pathetic flame. Real power flared by itself. Fire wasn't in their souls.

He stamped on other flames, beat them with his hands, crushed one blaze by slumping his whole body on it. The sharpness of the pain barely registered.

A lot of people came to see him. They smiled and spoke kindly.

'His drunken mother burned the house down when he was tiny,' said one. 'Imagine how that's affected him.'

'What about the foster parents?'

'It might have been an accident? He might have found the fire and tried to put it out.'

'He hoards matches, but he's done nothing but put fires out while he's been here.'

So he graduated into the world, into a hostel where he lived with others. He hoarded matches, kept his mouth shut and waited until it was time to open another door.

His job was stacking the lorry at dusk. One night, the driver told him to get in. 'We want a hand at the other end.'

The other end was a basement. He sneaked back there by day. It was huge, the midpoint of what must be the hub of the world, the busiest place he'd ever seen. It held shops and offices. It had trains and a hospital... churches with spires pointing at the sky. And all connected like a giant web from the murky basement.

He went on the lorry every night. Sometimes, they had to call loudly to get him back from the far reaches of the maintenance ducts. By night, he explored the web from below; by day he drank in the bustle from above. He worked out just where to spill the liquid that fed the power; just where to stand to be at the heart of it. Fire burnt bright within his soul.

It was time to open the final door.

About the Author

Penny is a prolific writer of both fiction and non-fiction and has won an international Crime Writers' Dagger for her crime writing. In a varied career that has taken her round the world, she has been based in academia, healthcare and the world of writers' rights. She was awarded her doctorate in 1992 and spent six years as Chair of the world's largest writers' organisation, the ALCS. She lives with her husband and sundry animals in East Yorkshire where many of her books are set.

Visit Penny's website at www.pennygrubb.com to learn more.

Music at Full Moon by Melodie Trudeaux

While we ate, the singing floated down the stairs. Nobody said a word.

Mary Two and I sat with Darren and Carl and made like we were all friends. It made the Sykes Twins uncomfortable, but I knew they wouldn't back down.

I hadn't planned it with Mary Two. I was surprised she had the gumption to do something like this.

I'd looked the question at Darren who'd whispered, 'I thought it was you, but Carl said it's Mary Two. She must have sneaked in early with her fancy new system.'

'Where's she put it?'

He shrugged. 'The Sykes Twins came in. We had to shut up.'

I was late. Deliberately. It let them know I was the most important one there.

The area was busy with kids out trick-or-treating, but they would steer clear of this place with all the stories especially at Halloween and a full moon.

It was extra spooky with Mary Two's music playing from up there.

The Sykes didn't go at their chips like they usually did. Nor did we. They'd said they would go up there. Full moon... Halloween...

And here we were.

If they got to the top and let their rockets off, we were going to look stupid. It was good to see them all jumpy, but it wouldn't stop them. Why should it? Like they always said, 'Just an old building waiting for the bulldozers.'

Mary Two's system droned out its weird music from up above us. No one said anything.

We screwed up the last of the chip papers.

I saw Dean Sykes take a deep breath. Then he nodded at his brother and they set off up the stairs.

They disappeared into the gloom, Dean Sykes whistling all the while. It sounded thin.

Mary Two had set the music just right. Not real loud but just enough. She looked worried. They'd wreck her fancy system if they found it, but all we heard was the footsteps and the music. No crash of Dean's boot.

Then it stopped. Silence hung over us.

And a gasp came from above. We all heard it. Dean Sykes.

When the singing burst out we all jumped. Underneath it came a faint tinkling of breaking glass.

Darren leapt up. 'They've broken out the back. Come on!' He and Carl raced out to cut them off.

I smiled at Mary Two, and we set off up the stairs. We'd beaten the Sykes Twins. They'd bottled it and run. I wanted a look at that system. I'd make a bit more of Mary Two after this.

'Where have you hidden it?'

I asked the question as I stepped onto the first landing. The music played on above us. From the tiny window we could see Darren and Carl racing across the grass towards the road. They looked all around them as they ran. I looked too. The Sykes twins couldn't have made it to the road by now. Where were they?

'Where did I put what?' Mary Two said.

'Your music system.'

Then I remembered that sound of breaking glass. Breaking glass? There were no windows left in this place. There hadn't been glass to break in here for years. What did we hear?

Mary Two is looking at me.

'Surely it's your system,' she says. 'When we got here, I heard Darren telling Carl. He said Mary must have hidden it earlier.'

I remember Darren saying, 'I thought it was you.'

All the time my feet are going from tread to tread. Up and up. The singing's right above us. It's been just above us the whole way. We should have reached it by now. It pulls like a magnet.

I realise that the stairs don't go up this far. We reached the top ages ago. My feet won't stop. I continue to climb.

Then the music stops.

I hear Mary Two gasp. Just like I heard Dean Sykes.

And before I can turn, the singing swells up from way down below.

About the Author

Melodie writes horror stories, science fiction and stories for children. She is mad about horses and space travel. Her first published novel, Horse of a Different Colour, was dedicated to astronauts including all who had visited the International Space Station at the time of publication.

You can find Melodie on Facebook and Twitter.

From the Depths by Chris Chambers

Five hours before the green reaches our walls and we stand, transfixed, eyes trained on the murky, emerald shine of the ooze. It creeps towards us from all sides. In the overcast half-light of the afternoon, we fancy we can see the thing advancing but can never be sure. To stare too long into its depths tempts madness.

John Bideson sits quiet now on a stack of local advertisers, head cradled in his hands. He has calmed down somewhat from half an hour ago, Alan Clarke's blood dried to no more than a crust on his fist. No one can blame Johnny for acting the way he did; we all watched his brother leave the Post Office and climb the nearest car bonnet, the green sickness only half way across the car park back then. Paul Bideson had made it to the third car, using the tops as stepping-stones, before he slipped and fell in. Some of us believe we saw him dissolve beneath the murky depths.

All of us heard him scream.

Two and a half hours before, and little Lucy Cartwright tugs at my jeans. I am standing by the chiller cabinet, nibbling at a chicken and mushroom pasty. The pastry tastes dry, the meat no more than dead, processed chunks.

'Will we get out, Dan?' she asks, eyes glistening soft with tears and childlike hope. 'Mummy doesn't think we will.'

'We'll find a way, sweetheart,' I lie. Lucy's mum is still at the Post Office kiosk, bopping her head softly against the glass. Part of me wonders if the woman will ever be right in the head again even if we do find salvation.

An hour before the green reaches our walls and those of us still able to speak sit in the room out back and consider our options. We crouch there in the pokey storage space like six ne'er-do-wells shooting craps.

'How do we know?' Mike Calzetti asks. He still wears his meat-streaked butcher's apron. 'How do we know unless we try? Unless we help ourselves?' His Italian accent shines through under the stress and *help* becomes '*elp*.

Tommy the local paperboy sneers. 'You want to give it a try? Because I don't. What's your big plan?'

Mike pipes down with embarrassment.

'He has a point,' I say. Iris Smith from the local charity shop raises an eyebrow in question. Phil and Ethan hold hands and stare at me with hope. 'It's a choice: we either wait here like trapped cattle for that thing to squeeze its way inside or we try to fight our way out.'

Tommy pulls off his baseball cap in irritation. The blonde locks that all the girls admire tumble over his brow. 'You know what will happen,' he says with a sigh.

'Yes, but do we?' I wipe the back of my hand across my parched lips and then button up my coat. 'What if the stuff doesn't get a chance to touch us?'

Mike stares at me from across the circle. 'You're mad,' he whispers.

Ten minutes before the green monstrosity finds us and I stand at the open door of the Post Office. Everyone has evacuated the front shop and is hiding behind the kiosk's bullet-proof windows.

I am alone, wrapped head to toe in layers of clothes. My eyes are the only thing visible inside a thick balaclava and hood. The sight of the pearlescent tide washes away any shame or sense of ridiculousness I feel. The thing rolls a mere six feet in front of me. I can hear it sliding, coiling over itself. I can smell chlorine underpinned with something cloyingly sweet. It reminds me of burnt toffee syrup.

I remind myself to keep my head up above the surface and climb as soon as I have chance.

'Don't go, Dan.' A voice from behind me.

I take a single look back at the sea of anxious faces and then turn and run for the green ocean that waits for me.

About the Author

Chris is a writer from Nottingham. He trained as an actor in London and later taught Drama back in the East Midlands. Chris has written a collection of short stories, a novella and is currently working on his third novel.

Find out more at chambone.blogspot.co.uk/p/flash-fiction-short-stories.html

Three-wishes Jack by Carmody Lanes

We laugh quietly because we're trespassing. The three of us reunited after all these years.

Izzy holds our three-wishes charm. The porcelain figure must pre-date the film by generations, but we'd all swooned over Patrick Swayze in Three Wishes so we named it Jack and built a mythology around it and the abandoned house.

'How dangerous is this place?'

Pan and Izzy mock, but I'm not thinking of the childhood make-believe evil that always used to stop us at the foot of these stairs. I'm thinking of dry rot and years of neglect.

We reach the top of the narrow staircase. The door faces us.

We never got this far but I remember the ritual. I wrote most of it. 'Stand close. Two of us touching.'

'Izzy first.'

Izzy gives Pan a thumbs-up. Pan and I hold hands. We all hold our breath. The ancient handle's stiff. It creaks as Izzy tries to turn it.

When Pan's phone shrills, it's cardiac arrests all round.

'Pan!' Izzy and I admonish.

'Izzy's here.' Pan laughs into the phone clicking it to speaker so Izzy's mum's voice fills the air.

She giggles. I laugh. Izzy's mum on Pan's phone still tracking our every move. It's like we're adolescents again.

Izzy smiles, twists the door handle and shoves hard.

The breath is banged out of me. Izzy shatters. I'm sucked into a silent void, tumbling through time.

We find out later the danger didn't come from childhood make-believe, but decay, badly-stored drums of noxious chemicals and the last straw of Izzy bursting through that door. The shock wave tumbled Pan and me down the stairs. It was Izzy's mum who mobilised help.

Ten days later our bruises are fading. We stand together by the closed coffin to say our last goodbyes to Izzy.

I leave; don't want to see Pan ever again.

Only two months later she's begging, so I return.

'My fault... I told her my wish.'

'It was bad luck, Pan. The wishes were make-believe.'

'I would have wished for my rent arrears. £2356. Izzy wished my wish.'

I remember the thumbs-up. 'Is that so bad?'

She shoves a letter at me. Turns out Izzy signed up years ago. It's not much of a policy but it's the only one that paid out – the trespass invalidated the others. Pan's the beneficiary. The cheque's for £2356.

Pan's on her feet. 'I haven't had my wish yet.'

'It's make-believe, Pan. Just a horrible coincidence.'

There's ice in her laugh.

The site's well secured now, but a nuclear bunker wouldn't stop Pan. We get to what's left of the house. We climb the drunken remains of the stairway. 'Pan, we can't.' I try to be gentle. 'We don't have Jack.' *We don't have Izzy.*

'Jack will have survived.'

And sure enough, Three-wishes Jack, that myth of our making, is lying on the top stair.

'Most of Izzy's still here,' she says. 'Hold my hand.'

Her phone shrills.

Pan holds Jack towards the void where we last saw Izzy. 'Let Izzy go home!' she shrieks.

'Pan?' Izzy's mum's voice echoes from the phone. 'Is that you outside our house? Come in, I'll make tea.'

My hand's in a vice.

'It's not me,' Pan shouts, a grin breaking across her face. 'Go outside and see.'

The coldest of ice shivers runs through me as her grasp relaxes. Her face turns to mine, elation shining from every pore. I can't breathe. Images flash. The rush of the void, that last sight of Izzy, the closed coffin.

I grab Pan, yank her to me, snatch the tiny figure and clasp it to my breast.

I still have my wish.

Time slows to nothing. A fraction of a second stretches out to reach eternity. The voice speaks from the phone. 'I must have imagined it.' The words are flat. 'There's no one there.'

The porcelain figure drops to the floor. I place my heel on its tiny form. Relief flows as I grind it to dust.

About the Author

Carmody's life as a writer revolves around developing worksheets for science classes, but now and again she likes to break free and write something completely non-scientific even though she ever so slightly disapproves of herself for doing it.

The Gnome House by Fortune Selles

'I'm Sandy,' said Victoria, 'and pushed for time. Can we get on?'

If he'd already met Sandy she was sunk but he let her in, unsuspicious.

Thick dust swirled in a shaft of sunlight. The place was filthy. No surprise it hadn't sold, even apart from *that* reason.

He was lucky to have a potential buyer like Sandy who'd practically paid the deposit and hadn't seen it yet. Sandy was booked to come at four. Victoria was on the doorstep at three-thirty. Plenty of time to do what she had to do.

Sandy had a way with things. She'd be on a shoestring budget without much time, but might pull it off, unless someone happened to have a record of the original. 'You don't mind, do you?' She aimed her phone and clicked its camera.

'How creative, darling!' she would scream, flashing the photos around. 'Can you believe it started like this?' Once the original was in front of people, the façade would crumble.

Image is everything!

But she had to be quick, couldn't wait for this old dodderer, so strode through to the kitchen. 'Will this lot be staying?'

He looked puzzled then nodded.

Neighbours?' she asked.

'Keep themselves to themselves,' he answered.

She turned away to hide a smile as she headed for the stairs. Could he really think she didn't know?

Not waiting for an invitation, she marched into the bedroom whose window would overlook the garden – and the gnomes. A good clear shot of those gnomes would ruin forever any chance of a sophisticated ambience for evening parties.

But she'd got it wrong. It was a small windowless bathroom that didn't smell too good. Pulling a face, she withdrew.

'Come and see the front bedroom.' The man belatedly took charge.

'Tell me more about the neighbours,' she said.

'They're quiet.'

Good reply. She'd have done the same in his place, kept a cloak over the real reason he wanted out of the Gnome House. It had been a long time ago, maybe he thought she really didn't know.

Sandy knew... wasn't letting it bother her. She had a touching faith that a jury never got it wrong.

'What does he do?' Victoria continued to goad.

'Who?'

'The neighbour.'

'Which one?'

'Oh… I don't know… either.'

'One of them gardens a bit.'

She looked down to hide a grin. Gardens a bit! Police ever dig over the entire plot, she wanted to ask. Not that they'd found anything.

He was supposed to have murdered them in his darkroom. That would be in the cellar. She wondered if this house had a cellar. What would Sandy do with a cellar? Something light and airy, based on the work of some designer no-one had ever heard of.

They hadn't found anything in the cellar next-door. All they had was a confession later retracted, saying Providence delivered his victims.

'Do they have a cellar next-door?'

The man looked startled.

'I… uh… was just wondering,' Victoria amended, 'if all the houses have cellars.'

'I don't think any of them do.'

Good answer again. His house might be filthy, but he knew to be wary about the neighbours.

'Just the back bedroom and the bathroom,' he said. 'Then you'll have seen all there is to see.'

She marched through. This was the view she wanted. Time was getting on. She was cutting it fine. It would ruin the game if Sandy arrived before she left, after all the trouble of making sure no-one knew where she was. She had to get the gnomes. Sandy might laugh off the rest of it, but not the gnomes.

'I've already seen the bathroom,' she said over her shoulder as she raised the camera and stepped up into the window.

Gnomes filled the viewfinder. Big, little, standing, sitting, fishing... Her finger froze on the button.

Sandy was out there. Out in amongst all those gnomes. Sandy... in the garden next-door.

A voice behind her said, 'That wasn't the bathroom. That's my darkroom.'

About the Author

Fortune writes long involved statistical reports for his day job and poetry for relaxation. He has always enjoyed reading horror stories but this is his first serious attempt at writing in the genre.

A Walk in the Wood by Mark P Henderson

Rocks and pebbles guide my footsteps through a world of bare frozen trees into the blue mist of morning. Without these boots I'd turn an ankle on the path. Between the rocks the soil is friable, crunching under heavy soles, an archive of long-fallen leaves and crumbled stones. The air is still and ghosts of decomposition hover among the aromas of winter dampness. The trees are mainly stunted birches, oaks twisted in the battle to survive in a hostile place, hunchbacked hazels and alders, and beeches that aspire to greater height despite years of numbing experience; a few bronze leaves cling to their lower branches. In the diffuse light they cast no shadows. Mosses, of what species I can't be sure, festoon the deformed limbs and trunks of the oaks and the tumbled boulders beside the path: emerald fur, wet and cold and dead. I wonder where the path leads, where my boots are taking me.

There is scarcely any birdsong, scarcely any sound at all save the chill grumbling of an unseen river and the unsteady crunching of my boots on the path. I tread as quietly as I can. Nothing moves except me. Then a cry fragments the silence, a rattling croak, an amalgam of laugh and sneer from a bird I've never heard before. It sounds big and hungry. I quicken my pace, risking a stumble or two. The cry comes again. Direction and distance are impossible to judge; the trees and the mist hide or distort every signal. Was the second cry closer than the first or was it further away? And this third cry – behind me? Or in front of me?

The way ahead is interrupted by the edge of a precipice. Beyond the chasm the path continues, or resumes: as far as I can see, the rocks and pebbles, the friable soil, the moss-clad boulders, the oaks and birches and beeches, are the same; same winter silence, same blue mist. At the bottom of the chasm the river rumbles, patches of ice tumbling irregular and sharp on its black surface. A narrow stone bridge crosses the gorge in a single span. It looks old and unstable: a mediaeval pack-horse bridge perhaps, or maybe something the Romans built two millennia ago that's scarcely been maintained during the intervening centuries. It presents an either-or moment of decision. I pause, feet unmoving. Either I cross the bridge and continue along the path or I retrace my steps, perhaps to face the owner of the rattling cry.

I step down to the single-span structure and advance one tentative boot. The bridge doesn't move. I take another step, and another, and another. Stone creaks. There is a small gap in the parapet where part of the stonework has crumbled and slipped. I can smell perspiration and feel the tremor in my limbs. Then the cry bursts forth again, much louder now, much closer. It comes from directly below me.

I run across the rest of the bridge and reach the far side of the chasm breathless and shaking. Behind me I hear stones exploding, crashing into the river. For a moment I close my eyes. When I open them again the wood is transformed. The boughs are bare not because it's winter but because they've been ravaged by fire. Every tree around me has been burned. Burned recently. Branches to my right and left are still smouldering, trunks still glowing red. The moss on the boulders is charred black, crumbling in the motionless air. The soil between the rocks on the path has been vitrified. It's slippery. I can feel the heat through my boots. The blue mist is not the cold dampness of a winter morning; it is smoke from a thousand burning trees.

The cry surges upwards again, from behind me this time. Close behind. I hear a sound like iron talons scraping the side of the ravine.

Boots like these were not designed for running along a treacherous path.

About the Author

After he retired from a career in medicine and university teaching, Mark Henderson moved to the Peak District of Derbyshire, England, and started to write fiction and to collect and tell local folktales. In addition to a novel, an anthology of short stories and other works, he has published a collection of 62 traditional Peak District stories and tells some of them on his newly-recorded CD. He's secretary of his local creative writing group and secretary of the local concert society, and he regularly delivers talks about his work as well as storytelling gigs. He currently has a comic fantasy novel and a collection of puns under consideration by Fantastic Books and has another complete novel manuscript ready for submission.

Website: www.markphenderson.com

The Pond by Denise Hayes

At first the children thought that the pond in the woods was their own secret place. They had tumbled out of the shadows and hushed depths of the forest into a sunlit clearing and there it was, shimmering and shifting and alive with birdsong and whizzing dragonflies.

For Tom and Betsy and Billy it became a favourite haunt. They paddled in its sun-warmed margins, trawled for glutinous frogspawn in the spring and poked sticks at the huge brown fish that slid slowly past just beneath the surface.

Then one day in mid-summer they arrived to find a stranger sitting on the far bank. It seemed to be a grown-up, so – worried that they might be trespassing – they crouched behind a wall of bulrushes and peered through. The strange figure was wearing a hooded jacket and had its head bowed slightly so the children couldn't really see its full face. Tom and Betsy were simply curious but Billy was scared. The figure's skin was too white, as white as bone. And even though the children stared and stared they could not see the slightest flicker of movement.

'Perhaps he's fishing,' whispered Betsy, 'and doesn't want to frighten the fish away.'

Tom shook his head. 'I can't see a fishing line.'

'I don't like it,' Billy said, shuffling backwards. 'Let's go.'

'Scaredy cat,' said Tom.

'You're such a baby,' said Betsy.

But they left anyhow.

When the children returned a few days later the stranger was there again in exactly the same position.

'Maybe he never left,' said Betsy.

'Maybe he's dead,' said Tom with a cruel sideways look at Billy. 'Tell you what, if he doesn't move at all in the next ten minutes, how about we go over and check him out?'

The minutes seemed to creep by and all the while Billy prayed for the stranger to come alive so that they wouldn't have to go up close to investigate. Even Tom was a bit spooked when the time was up but - committed by his own earlier bravado – he set off towards the pond's far edge with Betsy and Billy trailing behind.

As they got closer, the children could see that the hooded figure was not a real person at all but a soft-bodied dummy composed of bits and pieces of clothing that had been stuffed full like a Bonfire Night Guy Fawkes. It was supported in its sitting position by a broom handle wedged against a rock. Given courage by this, Tom rushed round to view the dummy front-ways on. For a moment his face was frozen in horror then he shook his head and laughed and said, 'It's okay. Come and look.'

It was easy to see what had startled Tom. Pushed inside the hood was a skeleton mask with dark cut out eyes and a toothy mouth stretched in a rictus grin.

'It's like a scary scarecrow,' said Betsy.

Tom frowned, 'Why would anyone put a scarecrow here?'

'Herons', said Billy. 'It's to keep the herons from taking all the fish.' He could tell that Betsy and Tom were impressed by his idea.

'So I guess it's a scareheron,' said Betty.

'Well it didn't scare me,' said Tom.

Despite this sign of grown-up activity, the children felt the pond was theirs once more. Billy had learned an important lesson.

He would be braver from now on. They would see he was no scaredy cat.

After a bit of paddling and dabbling for fish the children pulled a few scary faces of their own at the scareheron then waved him a silly goodbye and headed back home.

The pond was now left to its own secrets. Bubbles rose to the surface of the water and popped, a fat bumblebee hovered and buzzed above the water-lilies, and the scareheron turned its head and stared through hollow eye sockets at the place where the children had vanished from sight.

One day, perhaps, a child might venture there alone. And the scareheron would be ready.

About the Author

This is the fourth story from Denise to appear in this anthology.

She Sings Only at Night by Nathan Robinson

She's close.

I can sense her now.

I can't believe I'm going to meet her after all this time.

My turn.

Millions queue through the night for tickets, all for a glimpse on a faraway stage or blown up on the giant screens so anyone who's lucky enough to get a ticket can take in her beauty. Everyone presses in, but leaves a respectful few feet between the front and the electric fence that borders the stage.

The crowds outside are miles deep. The city empties into a throbbing circle around the arena. The multi-cultural masses claw over one another to get to her. The death toll rises after each show.

But her voice stops all of this. It's like cream to the ears, high and delicate like glass, tingling the spines of everyone listening. Speakers burst the action from inside the arena to the crowds outside and calm descends. Listening is free, but the arena charges those who want to be on the inside. Scalpers hike the prices up because they know people will pay anything.

Her voice silences the crowd as the curtain pulls up, then all eyes are on her. No one moves. There's no break, just one song into another in her strange tongue that can't be placed, that no one has tried to translate. People just listen.

No one knows exactly where she came from. Eastern Europe some say, others say Russia. Different people tell different stories. But they all start the same.

A club somewhere, no doubt drenched in noir as she steps on stage. She captures them all, and she goes viral.

More footage emerges from similar smoky clubs and her fame grows as the world catches on and more gigs follow in bigger venues. Her fame explodes as she conquers Europe, then the world.

She's never been known to give interviews, speculation becomes rife and she lets the papers say what they want about her.

It all adds to her fame.

But I'm here, I'm part of it now.

She's finished the set and left the stage, but afterwards she meets a select few.

There are kids and parents, teeny boppers, young men, old men, young women, old women, every faith, every creed. Metal heads, folk fans, pop fans, classical fans and the massive gay following that adore her like a queen all mix together with everyone else. No one cares, they're all goggle-eyed and here for her.

They say you get three minutes.

I'm sure that's how long my daughter got.

No cameras, they say. Don't even try.

They pick fans out at random and a security guard has beckoned me over and hustled me through a side door. I've been chosen. Like my daughter.

I can hear palms slap on the door behind me in protest at having not been chosen. The incoherent, angry shouts don't bother me as the burly guards lead me down a darkened corridor. They tell me I'm very lucky.

I know I'm lucky.

I'm lucky to have got this far.

We arrive at the door and I keep it cool as they frisk me, finding nothing.

The door opens and a young girl aged about eighteen stumbles out, two guards helping as her legs crumple beneath her. The stamp on her hand is smudging with sweat. Just like mine. Like my daughter's when she came home changed for the worse.

I know the girl's not star struck.

The media covers it up.

Like before.

It's more than an illness, and it follows her from city to city like a long shadow of dusk.

She's there in the room, lounging on a sofa. Up close she is more beautiful than I could have possibly imagined. Purring, she turns towards me, her predatory eyes weighing me.

The guards push me forward and I pull the thin, wooden spike taped to my arm and charge into the room towards her. It's the same one I used on my daughter.

With red lips, she smiles.

About the Author

Horror author Nathan Robinson is an invited contributor to this anthology. He lives in Scunthorpe with his twin boys and his patient wife/editor.

He has had numerous short stories published: www.spinetinglers.co.uk, Rainstorm Press, Knight Watch Press, Pseudopod, The Horror Zine, The Sinister Horror Company,

Static Movement, Splatterpunk Zine and many more. He is a regular reviewer for www.snakebitehorror.co.uk.

His first novel *Starers* was released by Severed Press to rave reviews. This was followed by his short story collection *Devil Let Me Go*, and the novellas *Ketchup with Everything* and *Midway*.

He writes best in the dead of night or travelling at 77 mph.

Follow news, reviews and the author blues at www.facebook.com/NathanRobinsonWrites or twitter @natthewriter

Ouija by Stuart Aken

It wasn't even a proper Ouija board, just some alphabet cards I used to help remedial kids who had difficulty reading. Laid out in a circle on the coffee table, a small tumbler inverted in the centre, and each of the four of us pressing a finger on the glass.

I'd invited the girls for tea, as a treat for their help in class. After the meal, I'd suggested they might like some fun. The Ouija board was my idea. They agreed: two fifteen-year-olds eager to impress Mike, my husband, with their sophistication.

He pretended to be bored with the company of the sisters, Polly and Molly, protesting he could be out in the fading light, shooting rabbits, trapping moles or hunting the otter he blamed for taking trout from the river. But the girls had arrived determined to show how grown-up they were. Short skirts and ripening cleavages calling for his attention. Mike was definitely not bored with them.

He was bored with me, though, and what he considered my confined life at school. Thought me too soft-hearted for my own good. Stupid man. And he believed I knew nothing of his secrets.

When he kicked the table leg twice in answer to the inevitable introductory question, I didn't react. But the girls did. There really was someone there. A second pair of knocks on wood surprised us all. The girls looked suitably impressed, but Mike's fake confusion didn't fool me.

'Go on, then, Polly, ask it a question.' He made sure no laughter showed in his voice or on his face.

A little wary, her trembling tones finally formed a question. 'Can we ask you things?'

I knew Mike guided the glass in the direction of 'y', 'e' and 's', watching their looks express their fear. Fun for him.

'Ought we carry on?' Molly's question was respectful, almost awed.

'Yes' again. All too easy for Mike.

'Is there someone you don't want here?' My question surprised him.

I spelt out his name, never letting on as I guided the glass. 'Oh! Mike. D'you think we should stop? Maybe you should leave?'

Tough man Mike shrugged. 'Ask it.'

The answer came back, 'no' to both questions, so we carried on.

He studied the frightened provocative girls, sitting opposite him. In a year they'd be sixteen; fair game. That would amuse him. He'd have them like he'd had some of my colleagues he'd charmed over the years. He'd want to impress the innocents, now he'd started the game of conquest.

I tried another question, unsure of my intentions. 'Is Mike in danger?'

The answer, 'yes', came unexpectedly. One of the girls must have done that. I glanced curiously at them but neither showed any sign of cheating, and both wore looks of shock at the response.

Unsettled, I suggested we should stop, but Mike was keen to impress his future victims.

'What sort of danger?' he asked, upping the ante.

'Tonight, you will drown.' The glass spelled out the answer, fast as lightning. Not me. And I was sure it wasn't the girls. Maybe

Mike thought it was funny and was controlling the game again, but I couldn't be sure.

The girls were properly scared now, and I insisted we should stop. We put away the cards and glass and, a little later, I drove them home.

As we left, Mike boasted he was off out to hunt. His powerful torch, fixed to his headband, would illuminate the rabbits he intended to shoot. Illegal, of course, but he didn't care.

He was still out when I returned home. Around midnight, I went looking for him, the lack of gunshots causing me to wonder, especially after that rather specific warning from the Ouija board. From the river, the powerful beam of his torch formed a beacon, shining through the clear, soft flow of the water. I studied him for a time, to ensure he was no longer moving, and only then did I call the emergency services.

About the Author

Stuart is an invited contributor to this anthology. He has written romance, science fiction, horror, literary, fantasy, erotica, thriller and refuses to be pigeonholed.

Writing without pre-planned plots, he composes text on the fly, sometimes sitting down with no idea in his head and turning out a short story in an hour or two of concentrated key-thumping. Character is his driving force and he loves the vicarious adventure that's possible via writing; living several different lives through those of his characters.

He and his wife Valerie live in the Forest of Dean.

Find out more about Stuart and check out his cornucopia of advice for writers on his website at stuartaken.net.

Number Thirteen by Linda Acaster

Mr Marshall had been late before, but tonight didn't feel the same. Tonight Sweaty Marshall was taking them on a Halloween walk.

The cubs were restless, trainers squeaking on the polished floor, as irritating to Simon as the beeps from Zigger's iPhone as he and Chaz played a game.

'Want a go, Numpty? Well you can't – Ha!'

Simon sidled to the radiators, long cold. Mr Marshall hadn't arrived and Reverend Laceby always forgot to turn on the heating.

He huffed out his breath expecting it to float white, but it was the white of a lantern he saw, a zombie in a long coat dragging its leg.

Everyone started shrieking.

'Boys! *Wait!*'

Reverend Laceby switched on the lights. The cubs recognised him and calmed.

'Mr Marshall can't attend so I'm leading the walk. I've even dressed the part!' He plucked at his coat and smiled. 'Who wants to go *ghost-hunting?*'

The cubs roared, flashing torches. Zigger showed the light on his iPhone.

'Be very quiet,' warned the Reverend. 'We don't want to frighten any ghosts.'

Chaz sniggered.

'Two by two or the ghouls will get you!'

More boys chortled. Simon tried to hold hands but everyone had already paired. The Reverend began counting them out.

One, two, buckle my shoe...

five, six, hit them with sticks...

nine, ten, dance from a string...

eleven, twelve, dig out a grave...

The lantern swung close. 'Thirteen, is it? Unlucky for some. Shall we even the numbers?'

Simon escaped the offered hand, running among the boys bouncing torchlights off headstones and pretending to be monsters. He wrinkled his nose against an odd smell, worse than Sweaty Marshall's socks, worse than wet dog.

With a click and a creak, the gate opened. They snaked through, Simon last and alone. As trees crowded in he elbowed up the line to feel more protected.

'Big step, tiny step,' called the Reverend.

The cubs altered their strides, echoing... *big step, tiny step...*

Simon laughed. No one joined in. No torches shone, either.

The Reverend sang, 'One, two, buckle my shoe...'

The cubs murmured ...*three, four, open the door.*

Simon shone his beam into glazed eyes. His heart thumped hard.

'Five, six...'

...*hit them with sticks...*

Noises erupted in the undergrowth. Something white shot between the trunks. Simon flashed his torch, seeing only brambles and jagged trees.

'Nine, ten...'

...*dance from a string...*

His beam caught a raggy thing twisting on a rope, and he drew breath to scream. A blow knocked him sideways.

'Get yer going, did it?'

Zigger was grinning. 'It's choristers, you chavver. The Rev teaches them. Come on, we're gonna jump him.'

Pushing aside boys holding hands, Zigger ran, his torchlight criss-crossing the ground. Simon raced behind.

That smell again, stronger. The Reverend ahead, carrying the lantern. Simon smothered his nose. Not wet dog.

He ducked down, shutting off his torch. It was Chaz's hand the Reverend grasped.

'Number thirteen! So glad you've come. It's unlucky for some.'

They'd reached the cobbled wall, gravestones waiting beyond the gate. A click, a creak, and the cubs were snaking through.

Zigger bore down. 'Let him go—!' The dark shape of Zigger folded into the dark shape of the Reverend. All three passed through.

'One, two...'

...buckle my shoe...

Zigger's iPhone lay bright in the mud, then its screen turned black.

'Three, four...'

...open the door...

Light roiled between the gravestones. Simon fought the urge to vomit at the stench.

As the cubs turned into the gate, he threw himself across the gap to squirm beneath the bracken. A click, and he shuddered. A creak, and he whimpered, clutching at a spongy log, trying not to breathe.

He had to breathe, had to smell – not the unearthly stench. Sweaty socks. He knew it was sweaty socks because the spongy log was a trousered leg.

Simon was crying, now. He didn't want to crawl back to find Zigger's iPhone, or tell the police that Sweaty Marshall was dead, and all the cubs were gone.

About the Author

Linda is an invited contributor to this anthology. She is an award-winning novelist and short-story writer, living on England's Yorkshire coast. History has always fascinated her, especially the day-to-day lives of people who never feature in history's grand recollections. Undertaking the research necessary to breathe life into these long-ago lives regularly throws up direct and eerie connections to 21st century living that she exploits in her fiction. On her doorstep are the locales of her much-acclaimed paranormal "Torc of Moonlight" trilogy.

Find out more about Linda on her website at www.lindaacaster.com.

In conclusion

So our horrorfest ends. We sincerely hope you enjoyed these stories and if you did, please let our authors know by leaving them a review on Amazon and Goodreads. If you enjoyed 666 you might enjoy our other anthologies such as Synthesis and Fusion. They are all available at the Fantastic Books Store.

www.FantasticBooksStore.com

Thank you very much for buying this collection and for helping out the Freedom from Torture charity.

www.ingramcontent.com/pod-product-compliance
Lightning Source LLC
Chambersburg PA
CBHW060432130626
46555CB00005B/2328